My
Fabulous
New
Life

SHEILA GREENWALD

My Fabulous New Life

BROWNDEER PRESS

HARCOURT BRACE & COMPANY

San Diego   New York   London

Library of Congress Cataloging-in-Publication Data
Greenwald, Sheila.
My fabulous new life/Sheila Greenwald.
p.   cm.
Summary: Eleven-year-old Alison, having moved from the affluent suburbs
to an apartment in New York City, tries to make new friends and come
to terms with the homelessness she sees all around her.
ISBN 0–15–277693–1
ISBN 0–15–276716–9 (pbk.)
[1. Moving, Household—Fiction.   2. Apartment houses—Fiction.
3. Friendship—Fiction.
4. Homeless persons—Fiction.   5. New York (N.Y.)—Fiction.]   I. Title.
PZ7.G852My   1993
[Fic]—dc20   92-44928

Designed by Lisa Peters

B C D E

ONE

"I guess it's tough for you, Alison." All of a sudden my mother was sympathetic. "Leaving your friends between fifth and sixth grade isn't easy, but you'll make new friends. There may be some right here in this building."

I didn't answer. I was looking at my reflection in the toaster. Along with everything else, I had just gotten the worst haircut of my life. "The Pinhead."

"Are you listening?" my mother asked.

"Friends in the building." I repeated her

words which proves you were listening, even if you weren't.

That morning when I had gone out to buy milk with my sister, Julie, we came up in the elevator with a person my age and her dog. If my haircut was "The Pinhead," hers was "The American Beauty." Silky sheets of yellow-gold fell down her back. Her eyes were green moons, and her jeans got tight and baggy the way they do on models but never on regular people. Around her waist was a belt with a kit attached to it. On the kit in big white letters were the words ENVIRONMEN-TAL INSPECTOR. As soon as the elevator door closed, she pinched her perfect nose with her fingers, rolled her eyes to the ceiling, and began to wheeze.

Right away I realized Julie had dumped enough of my mother's Chanel on her to obliterate a garbage truck.

"Asthma," I explained to Julie under my breath.

The elevator stopped, and Junior Miss America bolted out. "Allergy to stink juice, turkey!" she gasped just as the door closed.

Julie and I were so flabbergasted, we passed our floor.

I told my mother this.

"There, you see," she crowed, as if I had just proved her point. "If you are open to new people and new rules of the game, you will find that someone who seems mean is really nice. For all you know, this building is packed with friends."

It seemed to me that aside from one nasty eleven-year-old and her dog, our building on the Upper West Side of Manhattan was full of snooty lawyer-banker types who glared at us in the elevator and then took off on running shoes.

I looked down at my feet. If I could take off on my running shoes, I'd run all right— north on the West Side Drive, through the toll, onto the parkway to the Cross County, straight to the Greenhill exit ramp, past the town hall and the railroad station, across twelve lawns, four fields, half a circular drive, up six steps and then ten more to the second story and *my room*, where nobody *ever* called me "turkey."

3

"I know you miss Greenhill and having your own room (my mother's telepathy was A+), but we were lucky to find this place." She opened the door to the fridge, took out a yogurt, and pressed it to her forehead. It was a hot June noon. "Dad doesn't have to commute to that job anymore."

"Also, he doesn't *have* that job anymore," I reminded her, though I shouldn't have. It was a painful subject and the real reason we had to move. Life in the city isn't cheap, but it costs a lot less than what we were up to in Greenhill.

"He was lucky to find his new·job," my mother said, squeezing into a kitchen chair that was jammed into the tiny space called a "dinette." She opened her yogurt. "Lots of people in banking and finance never worked in their field again after Black Monday."

Black Monday was the day when the stock market nearly crashed. For our family, it had been Black Tuesday through Tuesday ever since.

"Give it six months," my mother appealed to me.

4

"Six months? In Greenhill I had eleven years! I had my swimming pool and tennis court, and the Rolling Rock Country Club, and Jessie and Rosemary and Tina—and our club, the A-Ones, that I organized and was president of!"

My mother's mouth turned into a narrow line. I guessed I had gone too far. "You'll organize new clubs and find new swimming pools," she snapped. "You'll prove to us that you deserve your reputation for being sensible."

"I got stuck with that reputation before I knew what it meant," I grumbled.

The smell of Chanel wafted into the room, followed by Julie, who was crying. "I can't find my boxes."

"What boxes?"

"The ones she collects from my soap," my mother explained.

"But they're empty," I said. "Most people throw them out." I didn't go on to say that "most people" had been me.

"Please help her find them, Alison," my mother directed me.

"Hey, Julie!" I clapped my hands. "Who needs soap boxes when we're so lucky to have this fabulous new life?"

They both stared at me as if I'd gone around the bend, but Julie did stop crying. I followed her into her room. It was my room, too, though we'd put a bookcase down the middle of it to give the impression of what we'd had in Greenhill: rooms of our own. Her side looked like Armenia after the earthquake. This upset me because I am tidy. There are other things that upset me. Here is one: People who don't tell the truth. "Hey, Julie," I said. "I threw your boxes away."

She looked as if I'd hit her on the head with a blunt object. "Even the one with the rose on it that smelled like roses?"

"Next time you decide to collect things other people throw out, tell me," I said.

Julie began to get red. "How could anybody throw out my boxes when they're so beautiful?" Her brow creased and her dark eyes fixed on my face. She seemed a lot older than seven, and she was waiting for my answer.

I didn't have one, so I was glad that the phone began to ring. In a minute my mother stuck her head through the doorway. "It's for you," she told me.

Saved! I caught my breath. Maybe it was one of the A-Ones calling to invite me to do something. They each phoned a lot the first week after we moved. But this week when I'd called Jessie, she was out and didn't call back. Tina couldn't talk for long because her father had to use the phone, and Rosemary said it was weird that I wasn't in Greenhill anymore. I agreed it was weird, and then we couldn't think of anything else to say to each other—and that was even weirder. When I had first told my friends in the club I was moving, they'd had plenty to say.

"Why?" Jessie asked over and over.

"Don't your parents like Greenhill anymore?" Rosemary wanted to know.

Tina just shook her head from side to side and said she wished I could explain it to her.

How could I explain it when I didn't understand it myself? Why hadn't my parents saved any money? Why had they gone and built a second house in the country with six bedrooms and five bathrooms and a swimming pool, thinking they would sell it and make a huge profit, when they didn't have enough money to finish it? Of course, they couldn't have known Mom would lose her job, then Dad would lose his, the real estate market would collapse, and they'd end up with two houses for sale and no buyers.

"We thought the good times would keep rolling," Mom repeated again and again.

"Yuppies," my grandma Rose had said. "They never considered the future. I can't fathom it."

Neither could I. So when I took the phone from my mother, I wondered if it would be one of the A-Ones calling to ask me *why*?

"Hi." It was a clipped new voice. "My name's Rochelle Braden. I'm going into sixth grade at Ogilvey and I live in your building. Mrs. Gleason told me to call."

"Oh great." I did my own version of her voice. (I do that sometimes when I'm nervous.)

"So I wondered if you were free now and could come by, I mean up. I'm on twelve. Twelve-B."

I was going to say "I'll have to ask," because in Greenhill my mother had to drive me to visit my friends, but instead I said, "Sure."

First I put on my new shorts with fruits all over them and the matching shirt. (All us A-Ones have the same outfit. When I wear it, I feel like an A-One.) Then I called into the kitchen, "I'm going to visit somebody named Rochelle on the twelfth floor. She's in my class at Ogilvey."

Mom came to the door. "What if she's the person you met in the elevator who called you 'turkey'?"

"I'll tell her I'm chicken, and then beat it."

My mother laughed. "Remember, we aren't in Greenhill anymore. Sometimes shy people come across nasty. When it comes to city rules, all of us have a lot to learn, including you."

Did I mention that something else I can't stand is when my parents tell me I have a lot to learn?

Out on the landing, waiting for the elevator, I checked my reflection in the mirror: Short freckled nose, dark brown eyes (like velvet, Grandma Rose says). Even the pinhead haircut seemed better. I was an A-One, wasn't I? We A-Ones are good at something and good to look at. Jessie has horseback-riding. Tina plays tennis. Rosemary is our dancer-actress, and I'm the swimmer. I gave myself a smile (nice teeth), and the elevator door opened behind me.

"Going up?" someone asked.

I felt so stupid to be caught grinning at myself in the mirror, I scrunched up my face, as if I were looking for something in my eye. But when I saw who the other person in the elevator was, I forgot about pretending anything.

He was what we A-Ones call an MAMP. That's code for Most Awesome Male Person. About thirteen, with silky dark hair. His green eyes slanted upward, making him look like he was maybe beginning to smile about something—was it me?

"Uh, did you have a floor in mind?" he asked.

I'd forgotten to push the button. For a minute I forgot the floor, too. "Twelve," I remembered in the nick of time.

The elevator floated up, and so did I. Who cared if Wheezing Beauty opened the door to twelve-D? She didn't know it, but I'd had the best ride of the week because of her.

TWO

The person who stood smiling at me was a funny-looking easy-breather. Since I was naming hairdos, I called hers "The Dustmop." She was small and wiry, with a sharp chin, thin cheeks, and big red glasses perched halfway down her pointy nose.

"C'mon in." She stood back so I could step into the foyer.

Actually, I wasn't stepping. I was still floating as a result of meeting an MAMP in the elevator. "This place is huge," I said.

"We had the walls knocked down be-tween two apartments and joined them," Rochelle explained. "That makes us C and B. What are you?"

"C," I said, realizing we lived in half of her apartment. I stopped floating.

"C is nice. It's got that view of the river."

"If you lean out far enough to practically fall." Right away, I wished I hadn't said that. "My Greenhill house was bigger than A, B, C, and D altogether." I wished I hadn't said that either.

"Your next door neighbor, Alexander Partridge, has the A and B lines on *two* floors. He made it into a duplex," she told me. "It's the biggest apartment in the building. They say it's fantastic. He's a designer, and he's head of the co-op board."

"I know." I didn't go on to say that he had given my parents a hard time. "You would have thought we were welfare cases the way he treated us," my father had complained.

"His daughter, Kiki, is in our class, but she's not in the building except to visit. Her parents are split."

I followed Rochelle through a carpeted living room, down a hallway, and into her own room. It was air-conditioned and icy.

"Clear a spot." She pointed to her bed, which was heaped with clothes. A duffel and a suitcase half full of stuff were stashed on the floor. If she wasn't planning a trip, she was a bigger slob than Julie.

"Are you going someplace?" I asked hopefully.

"Switzerland." She nodded. "Camp. I leave tomorrow. For just a couple of weeks. How about you?"

"Last year I only went to swimming camp for a week in California because my great granny was very sick, but the year before we went to Rome. We travel a lot."

"What about this year?"

I tried to look breezy. "So far we've moved from Greenhill to New York."

"Was Greenhill neat?" Her clipped, gravelly voice reminded me of an anchor on the nightly news.

"My house was old and really big, and I had a pool and a tennis court. I was right down the road from our country club, Rolling Rock."

Rochelle didn't seem to care where I came from. "No country clubs here." She yawned. "But lots of shops, and I love to shop." She said it as if loving to shop were highly unusual. "Incidentally, I like your fruity shorts. Are they Beelzebub?"

"I don't know. My mom got them." I was glad I had put them on. "I like your T-shirt."

"It's just one of my dad's," she said. "I mean, not *his* shirt, actually. His company's. Braden Duds." I had heard of them. She narrowed her eyes and tipped her head. "Why did you choose Ogilvey?"

"One big reason was the pool." I didn't tell her a bigger reason was the partial scholarship.

"We've got a good swim team." Rochelle nodded. "Are you good?"

"Last year at swimming camp, I was an orange . . . *um*, intermediate."

"Uh-huh." She examined her nail polish. "This orange is supposed to go with pink, but it clashes with every pink I have. It even clashes with orange." She took out some of her orange clothes and held her nails against them to show me what she meant. There was a pullover sweater to take to Switzerland and a pair of shorts. "I wish I knew who'll be at this camp," she said. "Last year my camp was almost a hundred percent jerks."

"Where were you last year?"

"Stock market camp." She gave me her TV interviewer look to check if I knew what she was talking about. "We learned about the market and financial investments and money management. If your parents talk about that stuff a lot, it helps to know what's going on in their world. Money is interesting." She giggled. "It buys you things."

In Greenhill, she'd have been the A-One who was good at money.

After Rochelle folded her orange sweater she took me on a tour of the rest of the apartment. Really, it was more like a house. She wouldn't let me see her brother's room. "He's a subspecies pig," she said. "I like things to be tidy."

"Me, too." I wondered if her being tidy

meant we had something in common. I wondered if it meant I could ask her about the MAMP I had seen in the elevator. While I was wondering, the front door slammed. Rochelle's mother came down the hall carrying two heavy packages filled with bolts of fabric.

"Mom, meet Alison Fox from eight-C," Rochelle said.

"Nice to meet you," Mrs. Braden said. Even though it was hot, she wore a hat and lots of jewelry. "I've got to change before I melt."

"She's a decorator," Rochelle explained. "She has to dress like that. They all do."

We ate ice cream in the kitchen, which was entirely white, and then watched a soap because someone who had been at Ogilvey was in it. Mrs. Braden tapped on the door and said it was time to "scoot over to Kute Klose to try on shorts for Switzerland." I knew it was time for me to leave, but I hadn't asked about the MAMP.

"I hope you enjoy Switzerland." I got up. "I'll see you when you get back."

Rochelle waited with me on the landing

till the elevator came. "Ogilvey is OK," she said. "The work is hard, and they expect you to do it. If you don't, they get weird. My advice is: finish assignments and avoid trouble-makers, even though that may be impossible. We've got 'Ms. Big Trouble' right here in this building."

"Who's that?" Somehow I was worried it was me.

"K.J. Kendal."

"I don't know her." I laughed with relief.

"K.J.'s hard to miss. She looks like Junior Miss America and acts like the panel of judges. She has a dog named Ralph Nader and calls everybody 'turkey.' "

The elevator opened.

K.J. and Ralph Nader were in it.

THREE

I was so embarrassed that K.J. might have heard what Rochelle said that as the door closed behind me, I couldn't look at her.

"Are you the one who's going to start at Ogilvey that the office called me about?" she asked.

"I'm Alison Fox."

"Rings a bell. What floor are you on?"

"Eight." I realized we had just passed it and I had forgotten to hit the button.

"You have to give the elevator a clue,"

she said. "It doesn't just know these things."

For the first time I looked at her. She was smiling at me. It was a friendly smile.

"By the way, I'm K.J. Kendal," she said. "Mrs. Gleason from Ogilvey called to tell me you were moving into this building and I should say hello. Since this time I'm not dying from perfume pollution, hello."

"That was my sister's perfume."

The elevator door opened into the lobby, but K.J. didn't get out. She just kept smiling at me. "I'm headed for the park. Want to come?"

Was she serious? "This morning you called me 'turkey,' " I reminded her.

"I call *everybody* 'turkey,' " she said as if it were nothing. "The park's not far. I mean, we'd be back very soon. Could you?"

I nodded and followed her out of the elevator. Maybe my mother was right: Someone who seems mean can be really nice. Maybe I did have a lot to learn about city rules, even from a troublemaker.

We went through the wrought-iron lobby doors and headed west to Riverside Drive with Ralph Nader pulling us along. It was like setting off on an adventure on which anything could happen.

"I found R.N. in the park two months ago." K.J. gave the leash a tug. "He was filthy and buggy. We took him to the vet and cleaned him up. He's a great mutt."

"We had a standard poodle," I said. "We used to show him."

"What for?" K.J. looked puzzled.

To be honest, that question had never occurred to me.

Walking with K.J. was like trying to keep up with a parade—or more like a one-person freedom march. She didn't seem scared or nervous about all the people on the street. She didn't even look over her shoulder. Her legs were long, so she moved fast, and her hair blew out behind her like a blond flag. She kept craning her neck to see the rooftops and the sky, holding one hand over her eyes to shield them from the sun. On the corner of the drive, she lurched to a stop and pointed to a cloud of dirty smoke billowing from the top of an apartment building.

"Polluters!" K.J. exclaimed. Like a flash she dashed across the street and into the lobby of the building. I followed.

"Where's the super?" she growled at the dark-skinned man with a long black mustache who leaned on the door frame. One of his shirt pockets said "Handyman"; the other had his name on it, "Eddie."

"You asked me that last time," the man said, yawning. "Why you wanna know?"

"He's poisoning my air." K.J. unzipped her black kit. Inside, each in its own foam-rubber slot, were plastic vials. They were labeled Acid Rain, Chlorine, Bacteria, Ozone, Water Tests, Nitrogen Dioxide. She took out the vial that read Carbon Monoxide and opened a black notebook. A folder containing instructions fell out. While the handyman and I watched, K.J. opened the vial. With a pair of tweezers she lifted what looked like a plastic-wrapped aspirin out of the kit. "Remove the test button from the foil pouch," she read aloud from the instruction page. "Reseal the vial and put it back in your pack.

Expose the button at the test site for four minutes."

"Hey! Slow down!" The handyman waved his hands over his head. "I just work here. You gonna get me in trouble!" He mopped his black hair off his forehead with a red bandanna.

"Tell your boss I'll give him a chance to clean up his act." K.J. held off from opening the test packet. "If I catch him again, I'll run my test and call the Environmental Protection Agency to report him."

"Right, sure." The handyman tried to look serious.

K.J. put the vial back in its slot and zipped up the kit. "This building is on my list," she said. "I could blow the whistle."

"Hey, you're really scaring me now."

We started walking toward the corner. As soon as K.J. thought the man couldn't hear, she whispered, "I really got to him that time."

Got to him that time? Didn't she know he was laughing at her? *I* knew and we'd just met. Rosemary and Tina and Jessie would have known right away. None of us would ever have talked to the handyman in the first place.

We crossed a broad street into Riverside Park, which runs along the Hudson River. I looked back at Eddie. He was laughing. I couldn't wait to tell my mother that K.J. Kendal was dumber about city rules than I was.

"Gleason told me you lived in Greenhill," K.J. called over her shoulder. "I guess you didn't have crappy air."

"No," I said. "We had a country club and a swimming pool though."

"Country club? Swimming pool?" She shook her head. "You're lucky you got out and came here."

Lucky I got out and came here? I put my hand on her shoulder and stopped her. "Are you serious?" I pointed at the trees. "The leaves on those trees are covered with soot. There's broken glass on the ground. I don't see any place to swim for miles around. Why am I so lucky?"

"Because it's real." K.J. shrugged as if the answer were obvious.

"Greenhill was real," I informed her in my I-am-talking-to-an-idiot voice. "Even if *you* didn't live there."

"Swimming pool? Country club? That's Fairy Tale Land, and if you don't know it, you must be Little Red Riding Hood."

"What's wrong with living in a place that's not real according to you?" I changed my tone. She was not an idiot. She was trying to make a point.

"Life," K.J. said slowly as if *she* were talking to an idiot, "is not swimming pools and country clubs. For lots of people it is broken glass and sooty trees and pain and suffering."

I tried to keep a straight face. Junior Miss America, co-op building, private school. "How would you know about pain and suffering?" I asked.

"If you've got your eyes open in this town, you can see everything." She waved her arms, gesturing to include the whole park.

I looked around. Everything? In Greenhill I saw people who were more or less like us—mostly well off, mostly white, mostly healthy and well dressed. Here I saw mostly

25

a mix-up—white people and black people and brown people. I saw healthy-looking people jogging in nylon suits with color-coordinated tights or shorts and running shoes, like the kind my father wore. I saw sick-looking people in dirty rags lying on benches. There were nursemaids and mothers with small children. I didn't know if I was seeing "everything," but I was certainly seeing a lot more than I wanted to. I didn't tell this to K.J.

"Gleason told me you swim," K.J. said, changing the subject. We both knew she had made her point. We began to walk again. "Sports don't interest me. People interest me."

Suddenly, almost as if K.J. had called his name, a person shuffled between us.

"Hey, girls, got any change? I'm hungry." The man's reddish hair was long and matted. His face was filthy. His blue eyes were muddy and red. He came closer and so did a really bad smell.

K.J. and I began to walk fast, pretending he wasn't there. I could feel my heart banging like a drum.

The man followed us. "I'm hungry, that's all."

"I don't have any money," K.J. muttered.

"OK, OK." He put his hands in his pockets and turned in the opposite direction. Even so, we kept walking fast till we got to the crossing.

I was as winded as if I'd swum a couple of laps. "We certainly didn't have anything like *him* in Greenhill."

"He's down on his luck and has no place to turn," K.J. replied.

"My father says some people like to hang out and get high, and they expect everybody else to pay taxes to take care of them."

"That man was homeless, Alison," K.J. panted. "No place to live, no family, no friends." We crossed the street, and walked out of the park.

"I can't imagine that," I admitted.

K.J. slowed her walk. "I can. Maybe you heard, I don't have friends, either." She glanced at me out of the corner of one eye. "I look like Junior Miss America and act like the panel of judges."

I stopped walking. "You heard Rochelle Braden."

" 'Princess Duds.' She should drop through a hole in the ozone layer."

K.J. was silent. She looked bleak. "I'm not proud that I ran away from that homeless guy," she said. "The truth is, he scared me."

"He scared me, too," I said. It seemed sensible to be scared.

We didn't say another word to each other until we were in the elevator. At my floor, K.J. turned her green moon eyes on me. "So be at my place, Penthouse-A. Dinner is at seven o'clock."

"How come?"

"Maybe *you'll* be my friend."

The door closed.

"Maybe," I said to the closed door.

Four

"City rule number one," my mother snapped: "You never leave the building without telling me first."

"You said yourself we all had a lot to learn," I reminded her. "I didn't know that one."

"OK, OK." She shook her head and stopped looking angry. "I didn't either." I was watching her dice carrots into a stew. "I'm glad you met one of your classmates at Ogilvey."

"I met *two* classmates at Ogilvey, and they can't stand each other."

"Life is more complicated here." My mother sighed.

"It sure is." I was thinking of the MAMP in the elevator.

"Judging from that grin, I guess you don't mind."

I hadn't realized I was grinning. "It's fun to be invited out to dinner all on my own," I said, making up a grin excuse.

Now that I thought about it, it *was* fun. I never knew anybody who had an environmental inspector kit and a dog named Ralph Nader and green moon eyes and no clue when people were teasing her.

Before I went up to K.J.'s, I looked in a drawer for a T-shirt with a good message. Something about Earth Day or saving the rain forest. All I could come up with was a shirt that said Plant a Tree for Rolling Rock. The tree was faded, and there was a hole under it.

Julie sat on my bed watching me try on the T-shirt. "You have *two* friends in the building," she grumbled. "I don't even have one."

"I'll bet you find somebody soon."

"Where?"

"There's a person right across the hall from us," I remembered. "Mr. Partridge's daughter. She visits him."

"Is she my age?"

"A little older." I thought I'd leave it vague.

Julie sprang up. "I'll play the piano loud so she hears. She'll come tell me how she likes my music and we'll be friends."

If Kiki Partridge was like everybody else, she'd tell Julie to tone it down, but I wished her good luck and went up to dinner at K.J. Kendal's in my fruity shirt and shorts.

The Kendals lived in the penthouse on the sixteenth floor. K.J. showed me some trees planted in tubs on their terrace. The view of the Hudson River stretched north right up to the George Washington Bridge. There were tables and chairs for eating outside, but K.J. said it was too muggy, so we went in. I'd never seen so many books except in a library. There were shelves to the ceiling. Also, they had loads of plants and flowers. The furniture looked like the sort of things my mother would have put in the housekeeper's room in Greenhill—leftovers.

Mrs. Kendal was sitting with her feet up in a deep chair in the living room. She was reading papers and making marks on the pages with a colored pencil. She glanced up at me, took off her glasses, and smiled. Her face was long. She had glittery blue eyes and curly brown hair that circled her head like a fuzzy cloud. "I have to finish correcting these proofs. One more page, and I'm a free woman," she said.

"She's a journalist," K.J. explained proudly.

Through a glass-paneled door I could see into the dining room, where the table was set for five people. Cooking smells were coming out of the kitchen.

Something else was coming out of the kitchen.

"This is my brother," K.J. said in such an offhand way you'd never know she was introducing the MAMP.

"Hello again." He reached out to shake my hand. "I'm Jasper, and it's time to eat."

"Hello again?" K.J. looked puzzled.

"We took a ride together." Jasper winked at me.

"Up," I added. I began to float again.

We all went into the dining room and took our seats around a long table. Mr. Kendal brought in a tray of serving bowls, which he put on a side cart. He was tall and thin, with a square jaw and brown eyes made bigger and rounder by his glasses. I was trying hard not to stare at Jasper, so I looked over his shoulder at the wall opposite me, where a bunch of photographs had been hung side by side in a row. The faces in the pictures were so miserable, I couldn't look at them either.

"Those are mine." K.J. pointed proudly to the photographs. "I did them for my independent social studies project last term. We had to choose something in our neighborhood to research. I chose the welfare hotel down the block, the Manderlay."

"I call those pictures the K.J. Kendal Diet

Plan," Jasper said. "It's hard to eat with them staring at you, isn't it Alison?"

Before I could answer, K.J. cut in. "Just because you don't want to look at them doesn't mean they aren't there. The people who live at the Manderlay have no place else to go. They've got no jobs or money or hope."

"How did *you* get in?" I wondered.

"I never could have done it by myself, but Mom's friend Hattie is a social worker and she took me."

"Hattie even got K.J. invited up to a room," Mrs. Kendal said.

K.J. stood and took a photo off the wall. She handed it to me. The face in the picture was of a pathetic toothless woman trying to smile. "That's Lola. She lost her job. Her husband got sick, and their house burned down. She had no place to go but the hotel. We got to be such good friends I invited her here to dinner." K.J. tucked her blond hair behind her ears and sat down again.

"You invited Lola to dinner because she was your friend?" Jasper asked in an exaggerated way. "I thought you invited her because you wanted to do an interview that would knock the socks off your class and get you A-plus in social studies."

"I didn't care about my grade," K.J. shot back. "I wanted to help."

"Oh sure. By popping in and out of the Manderlay with your little notebook and camera." Jasper laughed. "I bet those people have never been the same."

"I didn't just pop in and out." K.J. seemed close to tears.

"I notice you never went back." Suddenly, Jasper wasn't laughing.

"I'll go back." K.J.'s voice was high and wobbly. "Once I finish my report on the environment, I'll go back."

Mr. Kendal tapped his water glass. "Round one. Back to your corners," he said.

Mrs. Kendal turned to me. "Sorry, Alison," she said. "Every night is fight night at the Kendals'. "

Fight night? I had never heard of such a thing. At our house we'd had money trouble night and lost my job night—and lost my job *again* night—but never fight night. Fight night or not, the food wasn't affected. Neither was Mr. Kendal. He kept smiling while he spooned out our portions.

Mrs. Kendal praised him. "Henry, your dinners are the best." There was a herring salad in the shape of a herring, with olives for eyes. Then there was something in jelly. They called it "aspic" and said it was from a recipe of Gran's.

"It seems right to serve Gran's aspic on Gran's dishes," Mrs. Kendal said. The dishes were beautiful blue china. The bowls were polished silver and had belonged to Great Aunt Lucy, who hated to cook. "We sold most of them," Mrs. Kendal told me. "Silver is a pain in the neck to polish. With the money from one teapot, we bought all those bookshelves in the living room."

"Thanks to a sugar bowl and creamer, we've got shelves in our den," Mr. Kendal added.

Mrs. Kendal tapped her spoon against the bowl in front of her. "These are next to go. Just as soon as we run out of book space."

"But we use them," Jasper said.

"Because they're *there*," Mrs. Kendal replied.

I looked at the beautiful bowls. Was it possible the Kendals didn't know or even care about Every Day, Good, and Best china? Did they just use "Best" every day because it was *there*?

Mr. Kendal turned to me. "Tell us about Greenhill."

"She had a country club and a swimming pool," K.J. blurted out, as if they were some kind of disease.

"K.J. thinks I lived in a fairy tale," I explained.

"You mustn't mind her, Alison." Mrs. Kendal laughed. "She takes after me. She's very opinionated."

"Opinionated? What do you mean by that?" K.J. looked suspicious.

"You make judgments without information," her brother said quickly. "You don't know anything about Alison's life in Greenhill, but that doesn't stop you from insulting it."

"Did I insult you?" K.J. asked. Her voice was a whisper. Her eyes were huge. "I didn't mean to, Alison."

"It's OK." I thought she was about to cry.

"It's OK," K.J. reported to Jasper.

"It's OK because Alison is sensible."

"That's what my family says," I admitted. "I like it when things make sense."

"What else do you like?" Jasper asked.

"Swimming."

"To compete?"

"In the breast stroke."

"And you like to win?"

"Against myself. I like to set my own goal and beat it."

"That's what I like." Jasper said. "But it's expensive to swim in the city."

We talked about health clubs in the neighborhood and how much they cost to join (a lot), and Mrs. Kendal told us about a movie she wanted to see, and we all talked about the food and how good it was and the books we had read most recently. There were no more fights.

When dinner was over K.J. and I cleared

the table. More of her photos of the people at the welfare hotel were tacked to the bulletin board in the kitchen.

"Jasper wasn't always so hard on me. He used to be my friend," K.J. told me. "He used to stand up for me and fight with people who gave me trouble. It's just since he started eighth grade, he picks on me. He even picks on me for beginning next year's social studies project so early. He thinks I'm doing it for a good grade, but I'm not. I don't care about the grade. I care about helping people who are in trouble." Her head was bent and her hair fell over one cheek like a curtain, hiding it so I couldn't tell if she was for real. It was hard to believe she didn't care about the grade.

Once the dishwasher was loaded, we went to K.J.'s room. It looked like an office—a very messy office. A red file cabinet stood next to her bed, and two more supported the wooden plank that made her desktop. If one of her famous allergies were to dust, she'd have been hauled off on a stretcher long ago. It looked like she kept her clothes on the floor.

K.J. noticed me noticing. "My brother is the neat one. I'm not interested in being tidy."

"I figured that out," I said.

A corkboard with clippings and pictures tacked to it hung on the wall over her desk. There were photographs of the real Ralph Nader, Rachel Carson, and Rosa Parks.

"Those are some of my heroes," K.J. explained. "They all stood up for what they believed in and took action. None of them had it easy."

K.J. cleared a pile of grubby-looking T-shirts off her bed so we could sit down. She reached into her red file cabinet and pulled out a blue folder. The cover was labeled "The Manderlay." Underneath in red pencil was a huge A+. She opened the folder and flipped the pages.

"When I handed this in you'd have thought I started World War Three. There were people at Ogilvey who said my parents were bad to let me do it. Kids in my class said I was weird. But Mrs. Epsom, our teacher, didn't agree."

K.J. passed me the folder. "I don't care

what they say." She tossed her hair back and looked over my head at the pictures on the bulletin board. "I try to remember my heroes and how it's never easy when you take a stand. Nobody likes an activist."

"I thought an activist was somebody who went on protest marches."

"It's a person who fights for what they believe in."

"If you're a person who likes to fight, I suppose it helps if it happens to be for something you believe in," I said. I wasn't talking about K.J.'s heroes on the wall. I was talking about K.J.

"What do you mean?"

"The minute I met you, you held your nose and made a face. That wasn't exactly friendly."

"I was having an attack."

"You didn't have to call me 'turkey.' "

"*Turkey* is just a word." Without warning, the green moon eyes began to fill up. "Sometimes if I don't act tough, people think I'm soppy and they tease." She reached for one of the T-shirts and wiped her nose.

"So you act tough and insult everybody and then decide they're out to get you?"

"They *are*," K.J. said. "You'll see for yourself. When we start school and they hear about my report on the environment, they'll tear me apart again. All of them." She looked at me sideways. "Except maybe you."

"I won't tear you apart, K.J."

"You mean you'll be my friend?"

I wasn't about to go that far—not yet. "I mean I won't tear you apart," I repeated.

FIVE

When I got home my father was eating his late dinner. I told my parents about my visit.

"They sound like a bunch of oddballs," my father said.

Usually when he calls people oddballs, I think it's funny, but this time I didn't. I thought he was right.

My father frowned. He looked awfully tired. "Who let her do that project at the welfare hotel?" He rolled his eyes. "Those parents aren't like the kind of normal people we usually know."

"The 'kind of people we usually know' are 'normal' for Greenhill," I said. "I don't know what kind of people are 'normal' for New York City."

"We changed our address," my father said, "but *we* haven't changed."

This made me feel better. I was still Alison Fox: Founder and president of the A-Ones. The best at swimming. Good student and nice to look at (or so some people said), especially in the water.

"I wish I could find a pool to swim in this summer," I said.

"We'll check them out tomorrow," my mother promised, but her voice sounded vague. "I hear they cost a bundle to join."

Maybe *we* hadn't changed, but our bank account had.

When I got into bed, I couldn't fall asleep. I kept thinking about dinner at K.J.'s. I had never eaten food like that. I had never heard talk like that. Also, I had never met a brother like that. He made me feel I had to be not just on my toes but on my toe*nails*. I was glad I'd broken city rule number one. I was glad I didn't like being told who to make friends with. I was even glad I'd followed K.J. to the park.

The next morning after breakfast, I looked out the window. Rain clouds were blowing off and the sky was clearing a little. "Let's ask Mom if we can get her some new soap," I said to Julie.

My mother gave me money for two cakes of gardenia and a bottle of bath oil. She told me how to get to the shop. For Julie and me, it was our longest walk together through the neighborhood: four blocks.

Outside our building, Julie held onto my hand so tightly it hurt. "This is scary," she said when we got to Broadway.

The crowds on the street were like a crazy parade going every which way—young people rushing and old people dragging themselves along as if any minute they'd topple over. There were babies in carriages or swinging in pouches from their mothers' shoulders. There were drunks in doorways or lying flat out on the sidewalk. It was disgusting. A bent old woman was foraging through a garbage can on the corner. She was opening bags and taking out food and soda cans. She put the food in one dirty plastic bundle and the cans in another. On every block there were beggars —men and women, black and white, old and young—all raggedy and dirty. Some had spread used magazines and books and shoes out on the sidewalk to sell. The sidewalk was crowded because there were so many piles of wet stuff. Some beggars sat in doorways or stood in the middle of the street jiggling paper coffee cups and pleading: "Got any change?" or "I'm so hungry."

"Oh Lord, I'm starvin'," one man said to us.

Julie pulled on my arm. "Look." She pointed to a pair of feet sticking out from under a pile of wet rags on one of the benches in the middle of Broadway. All around the sleeping person were broken bottles and trash.

"Don't look." I covered Julie's eyes. "Just pretend they aren't there. That's what everybody else seems to do."

The smell of perfume was so strong inside

the store, I thought the scent would have put K.J. in an emergency room. Pretty bottles filled every shelf. There were stacks of little boxes full of bubble-bath oils and creams. Julie went from one tester bottle to the next, spraying and dabbing herself. We picked out my mother's gardenia soap and a bottle of bath oil and gave them along with money to the woman behind the counter. Next to the cash register was a can covered in a pattern of violets and filled with sample glass tubes of perfume.

"Can I have that?" Julie asked.

"Help yourself." The woman handed Julie the can so she could choose her perfume.

Julie shook her head. "I'd like the can."

"The can?" The woman laughed so hard her long cornrows shook. Each one of her braids had a gold bead at the end of it. The shiny beads glistened against her soft black skin. She took another empty can off a shelf behind her and handed it to Julie along with the package for my mother. "Will this one do as well?" The pattern on the can was lavender sprigs. It still smelled of the lavender bath salts it once held.

"Now I've got a start on my new collection," Julie said. "I never had a can before."

As soon as we were out on the street, she opened her can and stuck her nose into it, as if the flowery smell would protect her from everything on the street. "I hate it here," Julie said. "I want to go home."

"We are going home."

"I mean Greenhill."

I knew what she meant. "This is home now, Julie."

"What can we do?" she whimpered.

"I'll think of something." I tried to sound hopeful.

"Is this our fabulous new life?"

"Not yet," I said.

When we got back to the apartment, I saw a note stuck under the door: "Alison, come up immediately! K.J."

Before I even rang her bell, the Kendals' door opened and Jasper poked his head out.

"I heard the elevator." He stepped into the hallway and pulled the door shut behind him. "I want to explain about last night, Alison. I'm not as bad as I look."

I wanted to say I thought he looked fine.

"I mean, I'm not K.J.'s enemy. She gets into trouble and she doesn't know why. My parents don't stop her. She needs somebody to watch out for her. She needs a friend."

"Me?" I asked.

"You."

"I just moved in."

"But you're sensible and—" He stopped short. K.J. was clomping down the hall.

We stepped into their foyer, and Jasper closed the front door behind us.

"Hey, what's going on? I didn't even hear the bell ring." She glared at Jasper and then at me. "We have an important test to run." She began to buckle her environmental kit around her waist.

"*We?*" (Something else I can't stand is being ordered around.) "I never said I would go with you."

"It's going to storm again," K.J. leashed Ralph Nader and reached for an umbrella. "Perfect for acid rain testing. The trees have been looking terrible."

"I thought that was because of air pollution," I said.

"Air pollution is the same as acid rain, turkey." She tucked her umbrella under one arm and opened the door.

I stood still as stone. My throat was dry, and my face felt as if it were actually swelling up.

"So come on," K.J. called over her shoulder.

"I'm not a turkey," I said slowly.

"Huh?" K.J. frowned.

"Why don't you try respecting people," I said in my ice voice, "the way you respect trees? Maybe then you wouldn't have so many *acid* enemies."

I heard Jasper whistle air through his teeth.

K.J.'s frown froze into a mask. "It's just a word."

"It's just a word you *never* use for a friend."

Ralph Nader looked from one of us to the other, as if he were watching a tennis match.

"I'm sorry," K.J. said.

" 'Sorry' is just another word." I folded my arms across my chest. I wasn't going to make this easy.

"Gosh, Alison." K.J. tugged on her long hair. "I'm sorry. I mean it. I'll never call you 'turkey' again."

Jasper looked at me over K.J.'s head and raised his brows as if to say, See what I mean?

I took a deep breath. "Where are you going, K.J.?"

"To a pond in Central Park."

I went to call my mother for her permission.

"A pond in Central Park? To test for acid rain? Alison, is this supposed to be funny?" she gasped.

"Tell her not to worry—Ralph Nader will protect us," K.J. hissed.

"Don't worry," I told my mother. "Ralph Nader will protect us."

"How about Jacques Cousteau or Vice President Gore?"

"He's a dog, Mom."

My mother gave me permission, but when we got to the park I wasn't sure she should have.

A dark cloud hung over the lawns and trees, and the air was steamy. Except for a few dog-walkers, the only people in the park were lying on benches under plastic garbage bags or huddled with garbage bags or old blankets draped over them like capes. We followed a winding path that took us right to the lake. K.J. went down to the edge of the water, unzipped her kit, and took out the vial labeled Acid Rain. She opened the instruction sheet and began to read aloud: "To test for acid rain, remove treated test strip from vial with forceps."

K.J. carefully followed the instructions and removed the test strip, as well as the little color chart in the vial. "Place strip in water for two seconds," she continued. "Remove. Shake off extra water and immediately compare to color chart."

She leaned over the bank and dipped her strip into the brownish mess. "One thousand and one, one thousand and two," she counted, then removed the strip.

"Sweetheart, can you spare some change? I'm hungry."

All of a sudden somebody was so close to us I nearly jumped into the water.

K.J. stamped her foot. "Experiment ruined."

"I'm just so hungry," the old woman repeated. She was small and bent, and she pulled a shopping cart that was full to the top with dirty plastic bags. She had light blue eyes, thin white hair, and white eyebrows that looked like soft feathers.

"I don't have any money," I said.

K.J. dropped the useless test strip into the kit and zipped it up. "All I've got is a quarter." She took it out of her pocket.

"God bless you." The woman picked the quarter out of K.J.'s hand and stepped back, pulling her cart behind her.

We watched her follow the winding path.

"She reminds me of the welfare hotel." K.J. shuddered.

"How?"

"It was so awful there. Can you keep a secret?" She didn't wait for my answer. "I was really scared to go inside the Manderlay.

I had to force myself. It made me practically sick to my stomach."

"Why did you do it then?"

"If we're going to make a difference, we can't let ourselves get scared."

"What kind of difference?"

She lifted her eyes and seemed to be looking at something wonderful very far away. "I'd like to help people. Give clothes to the ones who need them and food to the ones who are hungry and houses and apartments to the ones who are homeless and medicine to the sick. I dream about those things. Don't you?"

"No." I shook my head. "I don't." I wasn't sure if she really did either. I tried to check her expression to see if she was putting me on. (My friend Rosemary can say things like K.J. says and even make her eyes go teary, but it's all acting.)

K.J.'s eyes kept shining. "I'd take that old woman home with me and sit her down in my room and fix her a dinner of everything she'd love to eat. Then I'd make up the spare bed for her so she could have a good night's sleep."

"I don't think you can do that."

"I know, I know. Even when I brought Lola home for my report, people in the building acted as if I'd gone nuts. Can you explain it to me? If somebody is without a bed, doesn't it make sense to give her one?"

I wouldn't want to give a strange, dirty person a bed in my house. I would never bring someone like that home. I didn't know what she was talking about, so I didn't answer.

It began to rain. Big fat drops fell on us. Any minute the scattered drops would turn into a torrent. K.J. put up her umbrella and yanked on R.N.'s leash. "That's why I switched to the environment. It's not so emotional. Maybe I can do something about acid rain without getting into trouble."

The rain came down in a solid sheet. It bounced off the paths around the lake. We began to run out of the park. The heavy rain fell on trees and grass as if it could flatten them.

The old woman stood under a tree watching us run.

Six

As I walked in the door to our apartment, my mother was hanging up the telephone. "I've been checking out the local health clubs," she said. "Using a private pool is pretty pricey. Health clubs cost five hundred dollars to join." Then she smiled. "Rosemary called."

I ran to the phone and dialed my old friend.

"My dad can pick you up on his way home from work tomorrow," Rosemary told me.

"Tina and Jessie are coming. We'll have a sleepover meeting of the club. How about it?"

"Fantastic," I said.

"See? You didn't move so far away." Rosemary giggled.

That's what you think, I thought.

By the time Mr. Dryden picked me up, I had packed and repacked my overnight case about five times. I wanted to look like an A-One, but even though I was wearing my fruity shorts, something wasn't right. I could just hear Rosemary say, "Oh, Alison, you're so New York now." Thinking about it gave me the jitters.

Driving out of the city, watching tall buildings disappear and smaller ones take their place, made me feel better. Once we went through the toll there were more lawns and trees—and more sky. I took a deep breath.

"Greenhill is a hard place to leave," Mr. Dryden said.

"A friend I met in my building says it's Fairy Tale Land."

Mr. Dryden laughed. "That may be true. But what's wrong with Fairy Tale Land?"

"She thinks it's wrong not to know about real life."

"You mean homelessness and all that?" He shrugged. "We pay taxes to support programs for the poor. How much more can we do?"

"My friend thinks we should know about it, even if we can't do anything about it," I said.

"What do you think, Alison?"

I remembered what my father used to say when he had to keep paying his taxes even though he'd lost his job and was running out of money. "My father always says that some people just want to hang out and get high and let other people pay their way. I think he's right."

Mr. Dryden took one hand off the steering wheel and rumpled my pinhead hairdo. "Who would ever guess that under that pretty head of yours there were such serious thoughts?"

Even though he meant to compliment me, I didn't feel better. If my head was "pretty," was that a reason for it not to have serious thoughts? "Until we moved, I didn't know about these things," I said. "Now that I know, I can't pretend I don't."

When we got to Rosemary's, Tina and Jessie were already there, along with someone new. Her name was Lisa and she had just moved to Greenhill from upstate.

"Lisa has the best pool you ever saw," Jessie gushed. "And you'll never guess what she collects!"

I had a feeling she was collecting my old friends.

"I collect perfume bottles," Lisa said. "My aunt sent me one from France that has a real amethyst stopper."

I thought of Julie and her cardboard soap boxes. Pathetic.

Lisa had long red hair pulled back in a barrette. She had very smooth skin and deep blue eyes. She looked like an old-fashioned wax doll. We A-Ones all got great tans. I could just see her covered with sun blisters.

"Lisa has a horse," Jessie said.

"Well, I *hope* I have a horse." Lisa shook her head from side to side. "We need to find a place to board him before we move him from upstate. We're looking for a really good paddock where he can stay until we build him one on our property."

I guessed this was her way of telling us she was A-One at horseback riding.

Rosemary put our spaghetti dinners in the microwave. "What are you frowning about?" she asked me.

"I was just thinking of my new friend in the city. She wears a kit around her waist that's full of stuff to test the environment. She'd probably be testing the kitchen right now for low-level radiation from the microwave."

"Weird." Tina rolled her eyes. "What does she look like?"

"A knockout," I said. "And her brother's a MAMP."

Rosemary and Tina and Jessie all leaned toward me over the table. "Is he an Impossible?" Tina asked.

"What's an MAMP? What's an Impossible?" Lisa was confused.

"Impossibles." Jessie cleared her throat. "Rock stars, athletes, ninth graders, and

MAMPs—Most Awesome Male Persons. You know, people who don't know we are alive."

"Does he know you're alive?" Jessie whispered.

"He asked me to watch out for his sister," I said.

"Like a baby-sitter?" Tina frowned and shook her head. "He's an Impossible, all right."

When the microwave dinners were ready, we put them on trays and brought them to the table in the breakfast room.

Jessie took a forkful and then pushed her plate away. "I'll never get skinny if I eat this."

Lisa twirled one string of spaghetti around and around. "One thing I hate is to be fat," she said. "Ever since we moved, I can't stop eating."

"It's hard to move, isn't it?" I said to her.

She nodded. "I'll feel a lot better when Twinkle is here. I'm supposed to show him in a month."

I almost asked her why, the way K.J. had asked me about showing our poodle.

"I should be riding him every day," Lisa

said. "But I like our house, and the Rolling Rock Country Club is neat. How is it where you are?"

"There's no country club and no pool."

Lisa wrinkled her nose. "I *have* to be in a place where I can ride and swim. I like to be outside."

"Me and my new friend K.J. go to Central Park for walks," I said.

"Isn't it dangerous?"

"There are homeless people and beggars . . . ," I began. "But—"

"Oh, I've seen that on TV," Jessie wailed. "When we go down to the city to shop, I can't look at them. Daddy says that's why we live here and he commutes. He says the city is no place to raise a family."

No place to raise a family? I thought of our new apartment, the beggars on the street, the noise, and the dirt. Maybe K.J. was right and it was real, but Jessie was right, too: it was no place to raise a family. I started to feel so awful I could hardly swallow my dinner. There was a lump the size of an egg in my throat. How come my father thought it was all right to raise a family in the city? How come I was the one who had to meet beggars and crazies every time I went for a walk?

Rosemary picked up our plates and dumped all the leftovers in the garbage, including the food Jessie hadn't touched because she wanted to get skinny.

"I've seen people in the street who beg for food," I said, "I've seen them look for it in the garbage."

"My parents contribute every year to this committee that provides food for homeless people," Tina said, as if soon the problem would be taken care of.

After dinner we watched a movie on the VCR in Rosemary's room. Her room has bunk beds and a sofa that opens out. The walls are covered in Laura Ashley roses, and the bed quilts match. She has a potpourri of roses on her dresser. It was like being inside one of Julie's boxes.

The movie was about a teen-age girl who lives in a poor neighborhood. She gets asked to a dance by a rich boy. The rich boy's friends are all jealous of the poor girl, and the poor girl's friends are all jealous, too.

"You don't belong here," the rich boy's sister tells the poor heroine. "Why don't you go home?"

I began to wonder if the rich girl in the movie was talking to me.

SEVEN

The next morning, just as I was about to leave, Rosemary put two dollar bills in my hand. "That's for someone on the street who's hungry," she said.

For a minute, I wanted to shove the bills back at her. I didn't need her money. Then I saw how her face was scrunched, and that usually meant she was going to cry. Rosemary is emotional. Being like that helps her when she's acting, but it can be a problem in every-day life.

"I dreamed about those people begging for food," she said.

I put the bills in the pocket of my shorts and promised I would buy food for somebody hungry.

When Mr. Dryden dropped me off in front of my building, he smiled sadly. "Take care of yourself, Alison," he said, as if he were leaving me in the middle of a war zone.

As I walked in, Jasper Kendal was coming out of the elevator into the lobby. A tall skinny boy was behind him. They were carrying tennis rackets.

"Alison!" Jasper noticed me right away. "Alison is K.J.'s friend," he told the tall boy.

"K.J. has a friend?" The boy gaped at me.

Jasper's face got dark. This time his eyes didn't look as if they were about to smile. "Why *wouldn't* she have a friend, Mike?"

"Because . . . you know . . . I mean . . . We all know K.J. and she's . . . you know."

"No, I *don't* know." Jasper turned to me. "Do you?"

Mike pulled himself together. "Your sister is hard to take, Jas," he said.

"Not if you get to know her," I said, and I meant it. Ever since I'd left Rosemary's, I couldn't wait to see K.J.

Jasper smiled at me, and this time I knew why. "She never apologized to anybody before you, Alison," he said. "She came back from the park like a different K.J."

"A different K.J.?" Mike yelped. "This I gotta see!"

"If you're lucky, maybe you will one day," Jasper told his friend, but he was still smiling at me.

Mike stood on one foot and twirled his racket. "So maybe if I'm lucky, we'll get going, Jas."

Jasper didn't budge. "Did you find a pool yet?" he asked me.

"My mother said she'd make some calls."

"I belong to a health club in a new building in the neighborhood. It's only seven blocks away. The Wellington."

"We'll check it out," I said.

"The courts will be closed by the time we check *them* out," Mike grumbled.

I watched Jasper follow his friend through

the lobby door. Was it possible he wasn't an Impossible?

When I got out of the elevator at our floor, I could hear the piano banging from our apartment.

"I don't have to ask how Greenhill was," my mother hollered over the noise. "You've got that famous grin."

"I could hear you in Greenhill," I yelled at Julie over the noise.

"I know she's there," Julie hollered back. "This will get her out."

"Me, too," my mother groaned.

When the doorbell rang a few minutes later, Julie ran to answer it. "I told you it would work," she cried.

But even before Kiki Partridge opened her mouth, we knew Julie's plan hadn't worked the way she'd thought it would.

"My name's Kiki Partridge?" Kiki said in a small voice. "We live next door?" (All her sentences sounded like questions.) "My Dad asked me to ask you to tone down the piano? There's a building rule about it? No playing on a weekend until after ten?"

Kiki Partridge was completely colorless, like an overexposed snapshot. Her hair was pale brown, and even her eyelashes looked faded. She was in my class, but she was the same size as Julie.

"I only did it because I wanted to meet you and have a friend in the building," Julie said.

"I told my sister there was someone next door who went to Ogilvey," I explained.

"I'm not here much." Kiki started to back away. "Actually, I'm leaving soon." She wandered across the hall, opened her own door, and something inside the apartment let out the sort of shriek you hear in horror movies.

"That's just Fruitcake." Kiki called to us. She opened the door wider so we could see what she was talking about.

Julie followed Kiki and I followed Julie into the foyer of the Partridges' apartment.

The ceiling in the living room was two stories high. A balcony wrapped around the top half of the wall. Plants the size of trees were everywhere. Vines hung from clay pots that were attached by rope to hooks over the windows. The room felt like a jungle.

"It's supposed to be a jungle." Kiki nodded as if she had read my mind. "Dad's new look is safari."

The furniture was simple—made of canvas, with bright pillows and rugs thrown over it. More rugs were hanging on the walls. A loud shriek made us jump again. A large bird with white feathers and a crimson crest glared at us from the balcony railing.

"Fruitcake would talk if somebody would teach him," Kiki said. "When I lived here full time, I bought a record that said, 'hello-hello-hello-hello.' My dad said it made him 'crazy-crazy-crazy-crazy.' "

Suddenly a tiny monkey with glinty eyes scampered over the transom of a door off the foyer. It swung by a light cord just past our heads and landed on top of a tall plant. He looked around for a moment and leapt back over the transom by the same route.

"Monkey!" Julie squealed, dashing after the monkey toward the closed door of the room.

Kiki ran to stop her. "We're not allowed in the studio," she said. "House rules."

"Do you have a room here?" Julie asked.

Kiki turned without a word and led us up the stairs and into a room off the balcony that was entirely blue and white. In the middle of the room, on its own stand, was a dollhouse. It turned out to be an exact model of the apartment, complete with ferns and plants and canvas chairs and jungle birds and other creatures.

"There aren't any people in it," Julie noticed.

"Not one." Kiki seemed pleased. "Who needs them? They just complicate things."

"Would you like to see our room?" Julie asked.

"If Mrs. Marshall says I can. She's my nanny."

Mrs. Marshall was in the kitchen cleaning the countertops. She looked as cool as the dark marble she was polishing. "Don't make it long," she said, glancing at her watch. I had a feeling she wanted to use her polish cloth on us.

In our apartment Kiki let out her breath in a long sigh, as if she'd been holding it for hours.

"We just moved" (my apology routine). "We used to live in Greenhill (bragging routine), where we had a huge house and swimming pool and tennis court, and there were these amazing lawns."

Kiki waited till I wound down. She never even looked at me, only Julie. "It feels nice here," she said.

Julie pulled her into our bedroom, and I went to the kitchen to fill some glasses with soda. When I came back to the room, Julie was holding up the can the saleslady had given her. "My sister threw away my whole collection of soap boxes—she thought they were garbage."

"My parents throw out my old stuff, too," Kiki said. "They like my things to be new and beautiful."

"Don't you?" Julie was fascinated.

"It's a lot of work keeping everything new and beautiful all the time," Kiki said.

"We used to have rooms of our own," I said. (More bragging routine.)

Kiki looked around at Julie's mess. "I wish this was my room." She gulped her soda. "I better get back. My mother is picking us up to go to the beach."

At the door Julie pulled on Kiki's hand. "Alison has two friends in the building, Rochelle and K.J. Now I have you."

"Everybody likes Rochelle," Kiki said. "But K.J. is trouble. You should keep away from her."

"Why?" I asked.

"She's always standing up for people nobody likes and things nobody cares about."

"What things?"

"Last year she did her social studies report on a welfare hotel. Her parents never should have let her. We're too young for that. It's none of our business."

"Why not?"

Kiki was turning a funny shade of pink. "Look, I'm just trying to warn you. Keep away from K.J. Kendal."

As I closed the door our house phone began to buzz.

"Meet me in the lobby in ten minutes," K.J. said. "I have to pick up some stuff for my mom at the deli. You have to tell me where you've been and what you were doing."

"You bet." I laughed. Keep away from K.J.? Who did Kiki Partridge think she was, telling me who to be friends with! I didn't even know her. Maybe K.J. *was* trouble, but she had ideas and thoughts and feelings that made her different from anybody I'd ever met. She'd asked me to be her friend. I *was* her friend—and I would have been her friend even if she didn't have an MAMP for a brother.

EIGHT

"What do you think of Kiki Partridge?" I asked K.J. on the way to the deli.

"She has a nanny," K.J. said, as if that were bad enough. "Also, she never opens her mouth unless it's to get me into hot water."

"What do you mean?"

"I'd rather not talk about it—it's past history." She grinned at me. "Tell me about your overnight in Greenhill."

"I'd rather not. It's past history."

"Fair's fair . . ." K.J. burst out laughing

and flung one arm around my neck in a cross between a hug and a punch. " . . . among buddies."

The deli was so packed we had to take a number from a ticket machine and wait for it to be called. I wondered how customers could decide what they wanted to buy. All kinds of breads and rolls in different shapes and sizes filled huge baskets. Cheeses and meats hung from hooks on the ceiling. Salads and more cheeses were stored behind a glass counter, bunched together, like the customers. Shoppers were milling around, some of them even asking for tastes. The food looked so good, and the smell of it practically made me weak with hunger. I put my hand in the pocket of my shorts to see if I had any money for a snack and found Rosemary's two dollar bills. After K.J. gave her order, I asked the deli man for an American cheese on rye. He included a pickle slice.

Outside the entrance to the deli was a man holding a sign: "Vietnam vet. No work. No place to live. Hungry." He looked it. His pale arms and legs flopped on the sidewalk as if there weren't any muscle in them. I handed him the bag with the sandwich in it.

"Thanks, sweetheart," he said.

"Thank Rosemary," I said.

"Thanks, Rosemary." He opened the bag and took out the sandwich. I stood and watched him.

"What's up?" K.J. asked.

"My friend Rosemary gave me two dollars to buy food for somebody hungry."

"Good for her." K.J. kept walking.

I stood where I was. I wanted to see the man take his first bite. He had dark hair and eyebrows like two wings separated by a crease. He reminded me of someone.

"These are heavy." K.J. shifted her grocery bags from one hand to the other.

I took one of the bags from her. "My father was in Vietnam," I said. I walked backward so I could watch the man chew and swallow.

"You can't take your eyes off him."

"He could be somebody we know." All of a sudden, I knew who. I stopped walking. "He *looks* like my father! Somebody should help him, K.J. He risked his life for us. He shouldn't have to beg for food in the street. We shouldn't have to give him sandwiches."

"It's part of the city scene we live with," K.J. said. "Like tennis in Greenhill."

"You're right." I slapped her on the shoulder, I was so excited. "I mean, it's not riding horses or swimming, but it's something we can do here."

"Give out cheese sandwiches on Broadway? Are you serious?" Her green moon eyes narrowed as she studied my face. "You're serious!" She shook her head. "That's a lot of cheese."

"So we collect for it. Rosemary gave."

"That's a lot of Rosemarys."

"There *are* a lot of Rosemarys. I'm sure of it."

K.J. thought about this. "Last year, I collected in the building for tree planting on our block. I got enough money for the committee to buy one tree and take care of it. I also got into trouble, as usual."

"How did you collect in the building?" I asked. I didn't want to hear about her trouble.

"Door-to-door, with a can."

"I know just the can."

We found Julie where I had left her, behind the partition in her part of our room. She was arranging her soap box and can, and a ratty collection of stuffed animals.

"We have an exciting project," I told her. "You can be part of it."

"How come?" She looked suspicious.

"Because you're responsible and act older than your age."

"And you've got that terrific can." K.J. reached for it. I could see why she wasn't famous for tact.

Julie put a hand in front of the can.

"It's so beautiful everyone will want to fill it with money," I said.

"You'll come with us when we go collecting," K.J. promised.

"You'll be in on the project," I added.

"What's the name of the project?"

"Dollars for Doughnuts," I tried.

K.J. scowled. "There's no nutritional benefit in a doughnut."

"Bucks for Bread. Change for Cheese."

"The cholesterol in cheese is a silent killer."

"The name of the project is Bucks for Bread," I told Julie.

She handed me her can. I got a piece of paper from my desk drawer and measured it to size. Then I wrote Bucks for Bread in red crayon, wrapped it around the can, and taped the paper down.

My mother looked into our room. She stared at K.J. "I'm Alison's mother."

"I'm her friend." K.J. jumped up and grabbed my mother's hand. "Katherine Jean Kendal."

My mother was so surprised, she took a step backward. "Nice to meet you."

"They want to go collecting with my can." Julie held the can over her head.

"Collecting what?" My mother looked alarmed.

"Bucks for Bread," Julie said.

"Is that some organization?" my mother asked.

"Are we some organization?" Julie turned to me.

All of a sudden, I got cold feet. "I don't know."

"Yes, we are," K.J. said excitedly, "and we better get going."

"Going where?" I thought for a minute my mother might block the doorway.

"Around the building. Don't worry, Mrs. Fox," K.J. assured her, "I've done it before."

"You have?" My mother didn't seem convinced.

"Are we really an organization?" Julie asked as soon as we were out in the hallway.

"We're *organized*, aren't we?" K.J. replied. "We'll start at the bottom and work up. There's no better exercise for your heart, and this workout is free."

It took me a minute to figure out she meant we would use the stairs instead of the elevator.

The building super, Mr. Alvarez, lived in an apartment at the back of the lobby. We rang his doorbell twice. "Nobody home," I said.

The door opened a crack. One black

shining eye blinked at us. "Nobody's home," a girl whispered.

"Aren't you somebody?" K.J. whispered back.

The door slammed shut.

"That's the super's kid," K.J. muttered. "She's always alone or with her mother. They only speak to each other in Spanish."

We walked up to the second floor and rang the A apartment.

"I'm not expecting anyone," somebody shrieked. "You have to go through the door-man and ring up on the house phone."

"I'm a neighbor, K.J. Kendal."

"The kid with the dog?" The woman opened her door. "What do you want now?" She looked from one to the other of us. She was in her bathrobe, and her white hair frizzed out from barrettes.

"We're collecting for . . ."

"Ice cream sodas, I betcha."

"When I collected for trees last year, the trees were planted."

"I never liked those trees—scraggly little

things, like weeds." She shook her head. "No, no, no! I don't keep cash around the house. Write me a letter." She slammed the door.

From the apartment across the hall we heard a beautiful voice singing scales. When we rang the bell the singing stopped. In a minute the door opened. A tall black woman in a silky caftan filled the whole doorway. She had coils of hair wound high on her head and bracelets up to the elbow.

We told her about Bucks for Bread.

"I'll give you five dollars and a piece of advice," she said. "Don't bother with the apartment across the hall."

As we climbed to the third floor, K.J. told us the woman was a great opera singer.

"She's got great advice, too," Julie said.

Nobody was home on the third floor. On four we talked to a cleaning woman who gave us a dollar. On five there was a baby nurse who gave us $2.50.

The tenants on six and seven were out. On eight K.J. said, "Why don't you ring Partridges' bell, Alison, since you know them."

"Who is it?" a woman asked.

"Alison Fox," I said. "I'm collecting for food for hungry people."

"Mr. Partridge told me the building doesn't permit door-to-door soliciting," the woman said.

"We live here," I said.

"I don't care where you live." The peephole clicked shut.

We climbed to nine. A woman carrying a baby on her hip opened her door. When she heard what we were doing, she gave us a big smile. "You're the hope of the future." She slipped two dollars into Julie's can. "Do you baby-sit, too?"

K.J. frowned at the baby. "No." She shook her head.

From the look on the woman's face, I thought she wanted to take back her two dollars. We weren't the hope of *her* future.

By the time we got up to the Kendals', Julie's can was full. We dumped the money on the kitchen table and began to count.

"Ten dollars and fifty cents," I said.

Julie ran her hands through the pile. "I'm a hungry person, too," she said. "Is that allowed?"

We were all hungry. "We have to sample the menu," I said. "It's allowed."

We ran all the way to the deli.

This time when we passed beggars on Broadway, I didn't feel so upset—I knew that soon I would do something to help them. I wondered if Jasper would think I was using other people's bad luck to make myself feel important. I wondered if he was right. I got so busy thinking about this that I wasn't paying attention to the order K.J. was giving the deli man till I heard him repeat it: "Tofu cheese with sprouts on whole-grain bread."

"Wait a minute," I said to K.J. "We have to have food people will want to eat."

"But they don't know what's healthy for them. Since they live on the street, they don't have time to read up on nutrition."

"How do you know?"

K.J. blinked. "I don't know." She turned back to the deli man. "A couple of loaves of

country white bread and half a pound of bo-
logna and a half a pound of American cheese
and—"

"A loaf of whole-grain bread and a con-
tainer of tofu cheese," I interrupted.

K.J. glowed as if I'd given her a present.

"I once heard that good business is based
on compromise," I explained. "It makes
sense."

NINE

When we walked in the door and my mother saw the bag of groceries, she got upset. "City rule number one," she reminded me. "You didn't tell me you were leaving the building."

"I forgot."

"That is no excuse." Mom's voice began to rise. "I never should have allowed you to go around collecting money from neighbors."

"Bucks for Bread," Julie crowed. "All in my can."

"We made enough to buy food for home-less people," K.J. put in.

"Food for homeless people?" My mother turned on K.J. "Why is it up to you to feed the homeless?"

"It was my idea," I told her.

"We just moved here and you're feeding the homeless." My mother was glaring at me now but talking to K.J., as if it were all her fault. "Alison would never have come up with such an idea in Greenhill."

"We didn't see homeless people in Green-hill," I pointed out.

"Now we see them all the time," Julie said.

"But it isn't your job to feed them."

"Whose job is it?" I asked.

"All day I have been trying to figure out how to pay our bills," Mom exploded. "The government ought to take care of the home-less. It used to. When I was your age, it did. I never saw so many hungry people with no place to live." She shook her head. "It isn't up to a couple of kids to run around making sandwiches. That is ridiculous."

All this time, K.J. and Julie were unloading the groceries onto the kitchen table. Julie grabbed some bread and American cheese and made a sandwich, which she took a big bite out of. "First one for me," she said with her mouth full. "Man, I'm starvin'!"

"Where did she pick that up?" Mom groaned.

"From people on the street," I said. "Shouldn't we try to feed them?" I opened K.J.'s loaf of whole-grain bread and started to spread the creamy tofu cheese.

My mother folded her arms across her chest and watched me. Her face was all creased up in a frown. Then she went to the shelf and handed me a fresh jar of strawberry jam. "A little of this would help." She took a knife out of the kitchen drawer and spread jam on a slice of bread.

When we'd used up everything we had, we loaded our sandwiches into plastic shopping bags and headed out to the elevator. My mother waited on the landing with us.

"Perhaps I ought to go with you," she said.

"Don't worry about us," K.J. assured her. "I know my way around the neighborhood."

But once we were in the street, I realized that knowing your way around the neighborhood was the easy part—it was knowing your way around the *neighbors* that was hard. Some people walked past really fast, as if they had lots of important things to do. They hardly looked around except to check the light before they crossed the street. Others lounged on cars or in doorways. For them the street was a place to lie down on and eat on.

The air was cool for a change. Bright sunlight made the sidewalk look cleaner than usual. Still, the garbage cans were overflowing, and every so often someone would fish through them, pulling out paper bags and checking for discarded food.

"I need money for my baby," a woman called out from where she sat in a doorway. The baby was in a battered stroller next to her. Both were white as paste, with stringy, dirty hair. I handed the mother a sandwich.

"I said *money*," the woman said. She ges-

tured at her baby. "She can't eat this stuff."
But she didn't give back the sandwich.

A black man with one leg hobbled over.
"Got any change for coffee?" He pushed his
paper cup in front of us. Julie reached into
the bag and handed over a sandwich. He
looked confused but smiled. No teeth.

A woman shuffled up in bedroom slippers
and said something in Spanish. A younger
woman who looked just like her was a step
behind. I gave each of them a sandwich. Three
small boys whom I hadn't noticed started pulling on the bag. I pulled back. They looked
like trouble. I gave each of them a sandwich.

A tall black guard who was standing at
the door of the welfare hotel yelled at them,
and they took off. Then he came over to us.
"I remember you from last year—the kid with
the notebook. What are you up to now?" he
asked K.J.

"Bucks for Bread," Julie piped up. "We
feed hungry people."

"Do you remember what I told you last
year?" the man said to K.J.

"You told me to stop hanging around," K.J. said. "You told me I would get into trouble. But I ended up writing a really good report for social studies."

"Maybe you got a good grade in social studies, but you get F-minus in common sense. This place isn't for kids like you." He turned to me. "There are people on drugs hanging around here and some who aren't right in the head." He pointed down the street to a low brick building with a white door. "That's the Uptown Interfaith Center. They've got a soup kitchen. You want to help out? Send them your money. They could use it."

"I went there with my class," K.J. muttered. "They wouldn't even let us in the dining room. All we could do was work in the kitchen, filling glasses with tomato juice."

"What's wrong with filling glasses with tomato juice?" the guard said. "Isn't that important enough for you?"

"I don't like to be ordered around." K.J. began to sulk. We walked away from the Manderlay.

Crumpled on the bench on the island in the middle of Broadway was the old woman we had seen in the park. Next to her was the shopping cart overloaded with bulging, dirty, plastic bags.

"Would you like a sandwich?" I asked.

"Hmm?" She smiled. "I'm just resting. I have a place to live now, but when I go out they steal my things."

I handed her a cheese-on-white-bread.

She tucked it into the top plastic bag. "Very kind of you," she said.

We crossed back to the other side of Broadway. Four small boys in raggedy T-shirts were banging on a gum machine in front of a newspaper stand.

"Don't eat that stuff!" K.J. boomed. "We have good food here if you're hungry."

I pulled out some sandwiches to show them we were serious.

"Do you have money for the gum machine?" one of them asked.

"I wouldn't give it to you if I did," K.J. said. "That stuff is bad for you. It ruins your teeth."

The smallest boy looked frightened. "How do you know?"

"Sugar," K.J. warned. "Watch out for sugar." She handed out all the sandwiches we had left.

"Could I have one for my sister?" the smallest boy asked. He looked younger than Julie. His face was dark brown and round and serious as an old man's.

"No more." K.J. turned the bag upside down to prove it. "But we'll be back tomorrow."

"We don't know that," I told her. "It's not fair to make promises if you can't keep them."

Out of the corner of my eye, I could see the boy was listening.

"This idea is too short-range," K.J. grumbled. "It doesn't go far enough. What's one sandwich?"

We started walking home. The boy followed us.

"Hey, José! Where you going?" one of his friends called after him.

"I gotta get a sandwich for the baby."

We walked down our block and into the lobby of our building. The boy was still behind us.

"Why does everything you do have to be big?" I asked K.J. "Can't you do anything small and simple?"

"Yes, I can," K.J. said, and then as if to prove it to me, she turned to the boy. "You come up to my place. I'll fix you a sandwich for your sister."

Two other people were in the lobby waiting for the elevator. One was the famous singer. The other was a medium-sized man with pale skin and a red mustache. He wore a dark suit, and in spite of the heat, he looked as crisp and clean as a mannequin in a store window.

"How did you make out?" the singer asked us.

"We collected enough money for lots of sandwiches," I said.

"Aren't they wonderful?" The singer turned to the man. "They collected door-to-door to buy food for the homeless."

"Collecting door-to-door is against this

building's bylaws." The man flashed a grin. His teeth under the red mustache looked almost fluorescent.

"Oh, come on, Al." She laughed as if he were joking.

When the elevator door opened, we stepped in and the boy followed us.

"Who's your friend?" the man named Al asked K.J.

"I'm not her friend," the boy said. "She's gonna give me a sandwich for my sister."

"We didn't have enough," K.J. explained.

"You're at it again, then. Even after last year's warning."

K.J. grinned as if she'd been complimented. "I got A-plus for that report."

"From your teacher, not from this building," he snapped.

When the elevator door opened at the singer's floor, she smiled. "Loosen up, Al," she advised. "You'll live longer. The kid didn't destroy our real estate investment."

He sniffed as if she had just given him an allergy. "We have certain bylaws in this building, Mrs. Ramsey—that is all I am pointing out."

The elevator stopped at my floor even though I hadn't pushed the button for it. The man tipped his head. "No more collecting, K.J." he said coldly. "It's a rule."

That was when I knew he was Mr. Partridge.

TEN

"What did you do last year?" I asked K.J. when the elevator door closed behind Mr. Partridge.

"I told you. I got into trouble when I collected for the trees."

I remember I hadn't wanted to hear about it. "What else?"

"That made Partridge mad, but when I invited Lola from the hotel up to our place for dinner, he had six fits."

I looked over at little José. *Seven* fits, I

thought. How could she be so breezy about it when it sounded so serious?

"I wrote up Lola's visit in my report on the hotel." K.J. continued as if she were telling a story I would really enjoy. "Kiki went and told her Dad, and he sent a warning letter to my folks. He said that if they couldn't control the kinds of people I was inviting into the building, he'd call a lawyer and try to have us bounced."

"Bounced?"

"Kicked out. Evicted." She reached into her pocket for her keys.

Even though it was a warm day, I felt a cold chill go right through me.

Jasper was in the kitchen heaping slices of meat onto a roll. "Who's your friend?" He gave José a suspicious look.

"My name's José." The boy frowned at Jasper. "I come for a sandwich."

"We were feeding hungry people on Broadway when we ran out of food," K.J. told Jasper.

" 'K.J. Activist' is at it again." Jasper rolled his eyes.

"It was my idea," I said.

"Bucks for Bread," Julie piped up proudly. "People put money in *my* can."

Mrs. Kendal came into the room.

"Meet José," Jasper told his mother. "He's here because K.J.'s sensible friend, Alison Wonderland, had an idea to pass out food to hungry people on Broadway."

I felt as if Jasper had kissed me and slapped me at the same time. Even though he said I was sensible, he said it in such a sarcastic way that I knew he was furious. But why?

"What a wonderful idea." Mrs. Kendal beamed at me.

"A wonderful idea?" Jasper hit his forehead with his palm. "Doesn't anybody around here remember the last wonderful idea that nearly got us kicked out of the building?"

"Now, now," Mrs. Kendal said. "I'm sure it won't come to that."

"You have to take risks if you're an activist," K.J. explained in the same voice she used when she was reading the directions from her environmental inspector kit. "You can't cave in every time somebody threatens you."

José was watching her arrange meat slices on a roll. "That looks good," he said very seriously.

I wondered if he knew *he* was the risk K.J. was talking about. "It is good." I smiled at him.

K.J. wrapped the sandwich in plastic and handed it to José. "Here you go."

He didn't say a word, just took the bag and headed out of the apartment. We followed him and waited in the open foyer doorway till the elevator came.

"Good-bye, José." I waved. "Glad you could stop by."

José kept his head down. When the elevator finally opened he hurried into it so fast he collided with Mr. Alvarez, the building super, who was stepping out.

"Is your mother home?" Mr. Alvarez asked K.J. He seemed really upset.

"Why?" K.J. blocked the door.

"It's very important that I see her." Mr.

Alvarez was small and thin, with a worried expression that got more worried by the minute.

Mrs. Kendal came to the door.

"I have to speak with you about a delicate matter," Mr. Alvarez began.

"Not another leak from our terrace." Mrs. Kendal groaned.

K.J. and I began to walk to her room.

"Don't go," Mr. Alvarez called to us. "This concerns you, too." He cleared his throat. "I've just had a call from the president of our co-op board, Mr. Partridge. He was very distressed." Mr. Alvarez took a notepad from his shirt pocket. "These are his words I wrote down." He cleared his throat: " 'Your daughter is entertaining an undesirable element in your apartment again, and by doing so you are placing other tenants and their property at risk.' " Mr. Alvarez put the pad back in his pocket and looked miserable.

Even in the faint foyer light I could see how pale Mrs. Kendal was.

"I wanted to talk to you about this before he brings it up at a meeting of the board next month. I wanted you to be aware of the situation."

"A meeting of the board?"

"We have many tenants in the building. They are very proud of where they live. They want it to be nice." Mr. Alvarez was almost whispering. "You remember how they gave you a warning last year and how unpleasant it was?" He looked gloomily at K.J. and then at me. "Maybe you can talk to Mr. Partridge and explain to him that he is wrong, that your daughter and her friend weren't breaking co-op rules collecting door-to-door in order to buy food for the homeless people she invites to your apartment."

"That's Bucks for Bread," Julie chimed in.

"It was my idea, not K.J.'s," I told Mr. Alvarez.

His big sad eyes rolled toward me. "You are the daughter of the new family in eight-C."

My face flushed so hot I thought it would burn off. "We just moved in. I had an idea to raise money to buy food for the hungry people we see begging in the street."

"You did?" His eyes opened wider.

"My daughter and her friend have a strong social conscience," Mrs. Kendal said quietly. "I am very proud of them."

"You are?" I could tell Mr. Alvarez didn't know what there was to be proud of. "I am proud of my daughter, too. But I must use discipline. I must guide her. We all must."

"Mr. Patridge is the one who needs guidance—*not* my daughter." Mrs. Kendal's voice was starting to rise.

"He is a difficult man," Mr. Alvarez agreed. "Always finding fault."

"I'll call him," Mrs. Kendal decided suddenly, "and do what I can to work this out."

Mr. Alvarez smiled with relief. "Thank you." He turned away from the door. "It's hard, a super's job."

When the door closed, K.J. looked at her mother. "You didn't mean that. You're not going to call him and work it out."

Mrs. Kendal put her palm on her forehead as if her head were really hurting. "Give me a minute. I have to think."

"What is there to think about?"

"We don't live on a desert island, K.J.! We live in a co-op. There are rules. I need to check on what they are." Mrs. Kendal went into her study and closed the door.

"Sometimes I think she's just like everybody else." K.J. glared at the door. "A do-nothing."

Julie pulled on my wrist. "Let's go home now," she whined.

"Home?" All of a sudden the word made me feel sick.

What had I done? What if Mr. Partridge really could get us kicked out of the building? K.J. was right. One sandwich to a hungry person on a summer day wasn't going to help anybody. It was short-range. It was dumb. Why hadn't K.J. told me about the trouble last year?

Why hadn't I asked her?

Eleven

My father came home early enough to have dinner with us. "I'm a meat-and-potatoes guy," he always says. Mom tries to slip exotic things into his food, which makes him suspicious. He fished a brownish cube out of his salad and held it up on the end of his fork. "What's this?"

"Guess," my mother said.

He put the mystery item into his mouth and chewed. "Marinated dish sponge?"

"Wild mushroom, Charlie." Mom laughed.

"Don't tell me—you picked them on Broadway."

"Four ninety-nine a pound. Still, I wouldn't be surprised if you *could* pick them on Broadway," Mom said.

"We picked up José," Julie said.

"Who's José?"

"He came to get a sandwich for his sister."

"A what for his who?"

"It's Bucks for Bread," Julie said. "We raised money for food and then we gave sandwiches out to hungry people on the street."

My father put down his fork and stared at Julie and then at Mom. "What is she talking about, Susan?" he asked my mother.

My mother stared at me. "Tell Dad what she's talking about, Alison."

I cleared my throat. "We couldn't stand seeing all the hungry people on Broadway, so we raised some money door-to-door for food that we gave away."

My father's eyes bulged. "Who's door-to-door? What food? Where did you give it away? What's going on?"

"Door-do-door in the building." My voice sounded like a whisper. "Food from the deli. We gave it away on the street."

"We collected money in my can," Julie continued. "But there wasn't enough food for José's sister, so he had to come up to K.J.'s to make another sandwich."

My father's face was stormy. "This building is a co-op. There are rules about collecting money door-to-door with a can."

"That's what Mr. Partridge says," I replied, hoping that since my father didn't like Mr. Partridge, he would side against him.

"I can't stand Partridge," he hesitated, "but I'm behind him on this. It's those Kendals. You've been seeing too much of them, Alison."

"Now, Charlie," my mother objected. "K.J. should have told Alison about the rules, but it was Alison's idea, so don't go overboard."

"Overboard?" Dad put down his napkin. "This whole city is overboard. I get on the subway in the morning and find people living in the cars. They walk up and down the aisles, begging for food, telling their stories. It's happening in every big city in the country. What are these people doing in the cities? Cities are expensive. Why don't they go live on farms or in the country? Why don't they get jobs? Because they don't want to, that's why. They only know how to hang out and cost money."

"Like me and Julie?" I asked.

"Don't be silly. You are just kids."

"So is José."

My mother shook her head. "It's not so simple," she said.

"Maybe it's not so complicated, either," my father said. "I lost my job. It was hard. We struggled. But I went out and pounded the pavement till I could find another one."

"We had a house," I reminded him. "We sold it. You said we broke even."

"Maybe you should make some new friends, Alison," Dad said. "What happened to that Braden girl?"

"She's at camp in Switzerland."

"I'm glad to hear some people didn't go

under in these hard times," Dad mumbled.

I noticed my mother hadn't eaten much of her wild mushroom salad. None of us had.

In the middle of the night, I woke up. My head was full of thoughts. I couldn't sleep. I kept seeing Mr. Alvarez rolling his eyes toward the ceiling. It made me angry that K.J. hadn't told me about the co-op rules. I fell asleep and had a nightmare. Mr. Partridge was yelling at my parents: "The board of directors of this building requests that you leave at once! Your daughter is no good!"

I began to cry. "I am an A-One. Best at swimming. Everybody in Greenhill knows it. I lived in a huge house with a tennis court and a swimming pool." When I awoke I was shaking. I wasn't an A-One and I didn't live in a huge house. We didn't even have enough money for my membership at a pool. Home was a small hot apartment we had to be very careful not to get kicked out of.

In the morning I was still angry with K.J.—but I was angrier with myself for not asking her what the "trouble" had been. I called her up.

"Bucks for Bread is dead," she said. "I have another idea." She told me to come right up to talk about it.

I thought maybe she had a plan to make everything up to Mr. Partridge. I should have known better.

When I got to K.J.'s she was in the middle of her room tossing all her clothes in a heap on the floor. "I'm giving them away. I don't need them," she said.

I wondered who did. They looked like rags.

K.J. flopped next to me on the bed, beaming. "This is so exciting. I mean, it's like my dream—to have plans to help people and make them happen. I always did stuff alone." She looked at the rumpled clothes all around her and then at me. "It's better with a friend."

Mrs. Kendal knocked on the door and peered into the room. "K.J., you can't give away all these clothes." She picked a yellow sweater off the top of the pile. "Gran knitted this especially for you, and it still fits."

"I want to give it away."

Mrs. Kendal sucked in her breath. "You can't do this. It doesn't make sense."

"It doesn't make sense to have more than I need. I'm going down right now to distribute these clothes on the street, and Alison is coming with me."

"No, I'm not," I said.

"Why?" K.J. looked shocked.

"It's another one-day idea that could get us into trouble." I tried to sound "sensible." "It's like Bucks for Bread—it can't work."

"Alison has a good point," Mrs. Kendal smiled gratefully at me.

K.J. glowered at her mother. I knew she thought we were ganging up against her. "Bucks for Bread was Alison's idea. Don't blame it on me."

"Nobody is blaming you." Mrs. Kendal backed out the door.

K.J. folded her arms across her chest and glared at me as if I had just stabbed her in the back. "Are you just jealous because this is my idea?"

"Jealous?" I gasped. "Of what? If you had

told me how much hot water you got into last year, I never would have gone ahead with Bucks for Bread."

"I didn't tell you because you were so excited about the idea, I wanted to help you out no matter what." Her voice was wobbling.

"Friends help each other out by telling the truth," I said.

"Friends." K.J. said the word as though it were an insult. She stood and turned so I couldn't see her face. She started loading her heap of clothes into a shopping cart. "I think friends are hard to find." She pushed the loaded cart out the door of her room and down the hall.

I followed her. "What are you talking about?"

"If we aren't going to be friends anymore, I'd rather be the one who ends it," K.J. said. "That way I don't get so zapped when you call it quits."

She opened the apartment door and pushed the cart out to the elevator. I saw wet tracks down her cheeks.

"When it comes to losing friends, I don't need to be a mind reader. I've been there, Alison Fox, and you have a lot of learn."

"There's one thing *you* have to learn," I said. "I hate it when people tell me I have a lot to learn."

She punched the down button to call the elevator. Her moon eyes had turned red as sunsets.

I didn't wait for the elevator with her. I took the stairs.

Twelve

The next morning I wondered if K.J. would call me to apologize. "She think's I'm so jealous of her idea that I'll dump her," I told my mother. "So she dumped me."

"K.J. has a problem with people," my mother said sympathetically.

"K.J. is the problem," I disagreed. "Everything she does is so extreme. One minute she's playing tough, the next she's crying." I thought of my good old A-Ones. Just thinking of them was like taking a rest.

I phoned Tina. There was no answer, so I dialed Rosemary but hung up after two rings. I didn't want to hear about Lisa and Twinkle. Who was I kidding? I wasn't an A-One anymore. I remembered how Jasper had called me Alison Wonderland. It had made me mad. He wasn't *an* Impossible, he was just plain impossible, like K.J. and life in New York City.

I headed off to the deli with my mother's shopping list. In the elevator was the woman who had asked K.J. and me to baby-sit. "I saw your friend out on the corner trying to give her old clothes away." She giggled. "Nobody wanted them. Somebody complained that they needed a good wash." The elevator door opened. "She's a funny one." The woman stepped out and wheeled her baby into the lobby.

I walked slowly to the deli, picturing K.J. packing up her clothes and taking them home. I wondered what was so funny about it.

The Vietnam vet sat in front of the deli with his sign and his paper cup. He didn't notice me. He was staring into space, glassy-eyed. Why was he asking strangers to give him food and money? Lots of people were in Vietnam. My father had been there, but he didn't go begging!

When I got home Julie was all excited. "Kiki invited me over," she cried as I came in the door.

"I don't get it," Mom said to me. "Kiki is in your class, but she's chosen Julie for a friend."

"She's my age and she's got a nanny." I realized I sounded like K.J.—not just her voice but her message.

I retreated to my part of the bedroom and tried to read one of the books on the Ogilvey summer reading list. I pretended I didn't care that Julie had been asked to Kiki's without me.

When Julie came home she burst into the room and pulled the book out of my hands. "Kiki always wanted a little sister like me," she said. "We played with her dollhouse the whole time. It is exactly like the real apartment—even the plants and the furniture."

"Is there a Mr. Partridge doll?"

"No, but there is a doll for each animal and bird." Julie twirled around. "Now *I* have a friend in the building. Just like you."

I went into the kitchen to find something to eat. My mother was busy on the telephone. I wondered if she was still looking for a job. "How can there be any work in real estate," a receptionist at one of the offices had asked, "if there isn't any real estate?"

"Still, we sold *our* house," my mother had said hopefully. "It was simply a question of offering it at the right price."

"Rock bottom?" the agent had guessed.

I was surprised when she hung up the phone smiling. "Get out your bathing suit, Alison. Grandma Rose's friend Mrs. Armbruster has invited you to use her building's pool."

"Can we afford it?"

"It's free!" my mother sang, as if she had won the lottery. "Free to the tenants of the building, like Mrs. Armbruster, and to their guests—you."

I ran to find my suit.

"Mrs. Armbruster will meet you in the

lobby of her building. She'll take you up to the pool and sign you in." My mother gave me the address. It was only seven blocks away. "Mrs. Armbruster will know what you look like from photos Grandma Rose gave her."

I always swim to the beat of a song. All the way to the pool I was humming a song I had heard on the radio. I didn't know the words, except the chorus, but I loved the beat. I could hardly wait to try it in the water.

Mrs. Armbruster's building was brand-new. It had a reception desk and soft, modern sofas in the lobby. Mrs. Armbruster was sitting on one of them. She was like my grandmother: short, gray, no-nonsense hair; rimless, no-nonsense glasses—and no nonsense. She looked me up and down. "You're like your photo all right," she said. "A beanpole." In the elevator, she punched the button next to the words "health club."

"The thought of all that athletic equipment makes me want to lie down," Mrs. Armbruster said. "What a waste, since I can use it for free simply because I live here."

At the health club desk Mrs. Armbruster

signed me in as her guest. "Your grandmother tells me you're part fish, so you better get into that pool fast." She waved goodbye.

Even though my grandmother thought I was part fish, I got winded on my first lap. I hadn't been swimming for a while. My muscles felt tight. My breathing was off. But then the beat of the song began in my mind, and I kicked to it and breathed to it, and I began to really move like the old Alison. I didn't care about K.J. Kendal. I didn't care about starting at Ogilvey or moving to the city—or anything. My thighs were working. My back stretched. I *was* part fish.

I swam one lap and then another. I put my feet down to touch the tile and lifted my head so water splashed around me. I felt sleek as a seal.

"You really *are* good," a familiar voice said.

It was Jasper Kendal talking to me from the diving board, where he was sitting, swinging his legs.

"I'm Alison Wonderland, remember?"

"I'm Jasper-I-Apologize." Jasper pulled up his feet and balanced in a squat at the end of the board. "I just couldn't believe K.J. would get us in trouble again after last year. I took it out on you."

"I didn't know about last year," I said. "And now K.J. isn't speaking to me."

"Maybe it's just as well for you. If you start Ogilvey with K.J. for a friend, you won't have to look for enemies."

"Is it that bad?"

He nodded. "I call it the K.J. Kendal Avoid-Getting-Hurt Plan. She was so sure you would dump her, she had to do it first." Suddenly he jumped into the water next to me. "Let's swim."

Swimming alongside Jasper was like doing some kind of dance.

"Hey, Jas!" Jasper's friend Mike called out to him. He was standing with two girls at the side of the pool.

"Who's she?" One of the girls pointed to me.

"K.J.'s friend Alison," Jasper said.

The girl whistled and rolled her eyes.

"K.J.'s *friend?* You've got to be brave." She was small, with zillions of freckles and little blue eyes. I wanted to smack her.

"K.J.'s OK," I said, imitating Freckles's voice, which was flat and toneless.

"Are you a member here?" the other girl asked me.

"Sort of."

"Oh, you got somebody to sneak you in."

"Yeah, just like you sneak us in, Betsy," Jasper said.

"It's supposed to cost a bundle if you don't live here," Betsy told him. "You're lucky you know me and I call you my guest."

"Betsy Bundle-Saver," Jasper joked.

"Betsy's Bargain Sneak-In," Mike added.

"Just be grateful." Betsy laughed as if she had meant it as a joke all along.

Maybe they thought there was something to laugh about, but I didn't. I didn't want to be "sneaked in." It felt like not belonging again. I couldn't wait to leave.

When I got home I told my mother the pool was great, but I didn't like being sneaked in.

First she tried to argue with me and then she changed the subject. "Mrs. Armbruster gave me the address of a terrific store called the Discount Warehouse," Mom said excitedly. "Let's check it out, Alison. We can buy your school outfits for half what we would pay at a boutique."

"Back in Greenhill you used to say you liked boutiques because their clothes had an individual look. You used to say you didn't want to dress like everyone else."

"Back in Greenhill I could afford to think I had an individual look because I was smart, when actually it was because I was able to spend a lot of money." She grinned at me. "Now we'll find out if we're smart enough to get that individual look without spending a lot of money."

I put on my fruity shirt and shorts. Julie wore a sundress that she loved. So now I wouldn't even look like an A-One anymore. I'd look like a person in marked-down clothes who got sneaked into swimming pools she couldn't afford to join. My mother's radar switched on. "Watch it Miss A-One." She winked at me. "Your self-pity is showing."

For all I cared it could hang out by a mile.

The Discount Warehouse was like a barn with racks of clothes where the cows would have been. It made me nauseous. I wanted to get out of that place. But my mother lighted into one of the racks like discount shopping was an athletic event she'd been waiting all her life to enter.

"I can't believe this." She snatched a turtleneck off its hanger. "The label's cut out, but I know this is a Kitty Belle—and it's less than half the regular price."

Julie and I watched. Julie looked as sick as I felt.

"Holy cow!" My mother held up a pair of fruity shorts just like the ones I was wearing. "I paid double this for yours."

"I always thought they made me look like an A-One," I mumbled. But all of a sudden, my shorts and shirt felt like junk.

"A-One is here." My mother tapped her forehead. "Not *here*." She pointed to her purse.

I caught sight of myself in a dirty mirror.

My pinhead hairdo was growing out. It looked like a fright wig.

Julie and I both ended up getting three new T-shirts and a pair of blue jeans. My mother bought herself a linen jacket and a skirt to match.

When we left the Discount Warehouse I was still nauseous. By the time we got home I felt hot and my throat hurt. All I wanted to do was get into bed. "Does self-pity make you sick?" I asked my mother.

"It doesn't give you a fever," she said, touching my forehead. She sent me right to bed.

I stayed in bed for the rest of the week. I read two more books from the Ogilvey book list. I watched a couple of soaps on television. I looked at magazines. I slept. Nobody called me. I didn't care.

I lay in bed and remembered how in Greenhill, when I was sick in bed, I could see the top of a magnolia tree outside my window. Beyond the tree was a slope covered with rhododendrons. In the spring the flowers were pink and purple. Now I was lying inside a small box with the wall on one side and the bookcase on the other and no air in between. Outside my window I could see the rooftop of the building across the street and a small square of dirty sky. I tried to think of something really nice for a change. I tried to think of swimming with Jasper.

By the end of the week my fever was gone and my throat felt better. I looked in the mirror. My pinhead hairdo didn't look like a fright wig anymore. It looked like real hair that I could pull back in a rubber band. I was hungry.

"You can go out for a walk," my mother said. "No swimming for a week."

The minute she said I couldn't swim, it was the only thing I wanted to do.

"But you complained about Mrs. Armbruster's having to sneak you in," my mother reminded me.

"This is a health emergency. Swimming will make me all better." Seeing Jasper Kendal wouldn't hurt, either.

She let me go.

This time I took my "paper suit." On the

swim team we called them "paper" because they're really thin and sleek and the best thing for meets. As I walked down Broadway, the beat of a new song started in my head. I couldn't wait to try it in the water.

Mrs. Armbruster checked me in. "You've gotten thinner since I saw you last." She eyed me up and down, and I knew she would report me to Grandma Rose.

"I've been sick," I said fast. I could just imagine my grandmother calling to ask Mom if we were getting enough to eat.

There were only two people in the pool and both looked like they were about Mrs. Armbruster's age.

I lay on my back and floated. Then I turned and did a few sidestrokes. Something splashed next to me.

"Hey! Where have you been?"

It was Betsy. Her black eyes and hair seemed blacker in the water.

"I've been sick."

"Summer virus." She nodded. "I had it for a week and a half. I hate lying around the house. My mother hates it more." She began to tread water. "Jasper Kendal's been looking for you almost every day. He'll freak when I tell him you were here. He says you're so good, you'll make the Ogilvey team even though you're only in sixth grade."

I began to like Betsy a little more. "Thanks. I work hard at it."

"Speaking of hard work, you made friends with K.J." Betsy's eyes got bigger. "That's like winning all the gold medals at the Olympics as far as I'm concerned."

"K.J. and I aren't talking right now," I admitted.

"Oh." Betsy looked as if she understood something. "So that's why Jasper's been trying to find you."

I began to like Betsy a little less. "I have to get out of the water now." I swam to the side of the pool. "I don't want to get sick again."

"Come back soon," she called. "Jasper really wants to see you."

Then let him really try to find me, I thought. *I am through baby-sitting an Impossible's impossible sister!*

I changed my clothes and went home.

Rochelle Braden stood next to a pile of luggage in the main lobby. She grinned at me. "As soon as I'm over jet lag let's get together," she said.

Her mother came in with the doorman, who staggered behind her with two stuffed duffel bags and a suitcase.

I'd been dropped by "Ms. Big Trouble." Was I ready for "Princess Duds"?

THIRTEEN

The next day Rochelle phoned me before lunch and asked me up for a sandwich. "You've got to see some of the stuff I picked up in Switzerland."

When she opened her door she twirled around in a cotton sweater that came down to her knees. The sleeves hung down over her hands. The pattern was like splashed paint. "How about this? Crazy, huh?"

It did look a little crazy on her scarecrow body, with her sharp face on top—a face that wasn't pretty, but one that made you want to keep watching. I was sure everybody at Ogilvey would try to find a sweater just like it.

"The kids were cool," Rochelle said. "I wish I could have stayed for another month. Now I'm back. What is there to do?"

We went into the white kitchen. She took a wedge of paté out of the fridge and retrieved a tray of bread all fanned out under a cover of yellow cellophane. "Leftovers from my parents' welcome home dinner for me," she said. There was a bowl half full of chocolate mousse. We cut slices of paté and spread them on the bread. "I hate this time of year." Rochelle nibbled on her sandwich. "It's like leftover summer. Nothing to do."

"We could take a walk."

She snapped her fingers. "We could check out the stores." She put the mousse back in the fridge. "We'll hit this later."

I called my mother. "Check out the stores?" She laughed. "What a great idea!" This was no acid rain test in Central Park. This was good old, normal shopping.

Rochelle knew her way around the stacks of bulky sweaters and bright jackets at Kute Klose. Sometimes she would stare hard at something and then snatch it off a pile or rack and hold it under her chin. She never checked a price tag. "Just looking," she'd tell any salesperson who said, "Can I help you?" She certainly didn't shop like my mother.

"I don't know." Rochelle dropped a pink turtleneck on the wrong stack. "Nothing sends me. Let's go home and try that mousse."

We started back to our building. "So what's been doing here while I was away? Did you meet anybody else from Ogilvey?"

"I bumped into K.J. Kendal in the elevator."

"Did I tell you about her?"

"You said she was a troublemaker. She says she's an activist who fights for what she believes in. She says she does things to help people." Why was I explaining K.J. to Rochelle as if we were still friends?

Rochelle rolled her eyes. "In first grade when some of us ate berries in the park, K.J. told the park attendant. We all had her to thank for having our stomachs pumped. She helped us, all right. Bad berries couldn't have been worse! In fourth grade, she brought a candle to school to light for Herbie Blecker, who got teased. She called it a human rights vigil for Herbie's self-esteem."

I started to laugh.

"Herbie was so mortified he stayed out of school for a week."

"She isn't like anybody I ever met before."

"That's the truth," Rochelle agreed. "The fact is, it's not easy being K.J. She's living proof that being smart and pretty doesn't make you popular. She sticks her neck out all the time but nobody appreciates it."

"She tried to give all her clothes away on the street," I said. "But nobody wanted them. She invited a kid up to her apartment and made a sandwich for his sister."

"My mother told me about that yesterday," Rochelle said. "I wanted to warn you. The Kendals could be in for it this time." We stood on the corner waiting for the light to change.

"What do you mean . . . *in for it?*"

"Al Partridge doesn't kid around. He got plenty steamed up last year after Kiki told him about K.J.'s report. This time, he told my parents that K.J. has to be stopped." She lowered her eyes. "He said you were with her, Alison. He said it was *your* idea."

The light changed and we started across the street. "It was my idea to raise money in the building to buy food for the homeless."

Rochelle's jaw dropped. "*Your* idea? Good grief! I thought you were Miss Polly Sunshine from the 'burbs. I never . . . I mean YOUR IDEA? Why?"

Why? It was my turn to be shocked. "There are hungry beggars everywhere you look."

"Don't look."

"But they come right up to you."

"Not to me. Not anymore. They used to scare me so much, it made me sick to my stomach. But I figured out what to do."

"What?"

Rochelle lowered her voice. "Watch."

A skinny man in rags stood near us holding

a paper cup in front of anybody who passed. "Got any change? Got any change?"

Rochelle pulled her mouth down and made a horrible face. She put her hands in her pockets and held her shoulders up around her ears. She walked fast and muttered. "Bug off, bug off."

The man moved away from us.

"See what I mean?"

I tried the face.

"Not mean enough."

I frowned harder.

"Better."

"Don't you ever want to do something?"

Her face changed again—to sad and serious. "Sometimes I even dream about it. I dream I make a ton of money designing clothes and set up a house, not like the Manderlay but really nice, where people can live and get help and straighten out." She pushed her glasses up her nose and squinted at me with interest, as if I were a stack of sweaters at Kute Klose. "Your mouth is open, Alison. I shocked you."

"You sound just like K.J.!"

"She calls me 'Princess Duds.' OK, I like clothes. Does that make me Imelda Marcos? Last year our class did a bake sale for the Uptown Interfaith Center. We went over to deliver the money and we worked in the soup kitchen. It was good. It wasn't my dream, but it was better than asking dangerous types up for dinner and having Al Partridge call his lawyer."

"They weren't dangerous types," I said. "K.J. has dreams about helping, too."

"No kidding." Rochelle laughed.

"Only when K.J. told me about that soup kitchen, she said she just filled trays and glasses with juice."

"Maybe it wasn't saving the human race, but it was something."

We walked into the lobby of our building.

"I mean, who wants to risk getting kicked out of their apartment?" Rochelle rang for the elevator. "The last thing this town needs is another homeless family."

"Another homeless family?" I knew she

was joking, but my insides dropped like a fast elevator to the basement.

"I can't wait to wrap my mouth around that chocolate mousse." Rochelle licked her lips.

"I can," I said. "I don't feel so good."

She squinted at me. "You don't look good, either. I hope I didn't upset you. I mean, I don't think anybody's going to evict your family over one incident."

"Thanks," I told her when the elevator stopped at my floor. "I appreciate that."

When I got home Julie was practicing the piano and my mother was on the telephone. I went into the kitchen and looked out the window into the courtyard. The windows facing me were like boxes, each framing a small stage. In one of the boxes I saw a man feeding a baby. In another there were plants hanging in baskets to the middle of the pane. We all lived so close together, side by side in every direction. How could I pretend other people weren't there? K.J. was right to want to help. Rochelle was right to want to help in a way that wouldn't get us into trouble. None of us could stand the things we saw on the street. All of us wanted to *do* something. Then again, maybe I had done enough. I'd set us up to get kicked out of the building.

I looked down into the lower window of Mr. Partridge's duplex. I wondered if I was looking at the room Kiki wasn't allowed to enter. A housekeeper was wiping the glass, so the blinds were up. The room seemed a million miles away from the beggars on the street. I could see a shiny wood floor and the corner of a woven rug. I saw the brass feet of a leather chair and the feet of an amazing statue of an animal with yellowish brown spots on his coat. Suddenly the housekeeper glared right at me and raised her hand as if she would shake her fist. But all she did was snap down the blind.

"I didn't know you were back," my mother called in. "How was lunch? How was shopping? Did Rochelle buy anything? Did you see anything?"

"She didn't buy anything. I didn't see anything."

"Thank goodness. We couldn't afford another T-shirt."

"I didn't feel too good, so I hardly ate."

"Before you start feeling too sorry for yourself again, you should know Jasper Kendal called. He asked if you'd call him back."

I ran to the phone. It never occurred to me that K.J. would answer it . . . until she did.

"Jasper is out," she said as soon as she heard my voice. "You don't have to be nice to me for his sake."

"It's not for his sake," I told the telephone. But it had gone dead.

FOURTEEN

That night Mr. Partridge called just as we were finishing dinner. When my father picked up the phone in the kitchen we stopped talking so we could listen in on the conversation.

Dad said "terrific" and "thanks," and then he came back to the table, glowing. "We're all invited across the hall for a welcome-to-the-eighth-floor dessert."

My father went to brush his teeth. My mother put on fresh lipstick. "I've been dying to see that place," she said.

Mr. Partridge opened his door. "Welcome to the jungle."

My parents acted like a pair of kids at Disney World. "What a wonderful space," Mom gushed.

"We live in a fabulous building," Mr. Partridge said. "Aren't we lucky to be here?"

Lucky to be here? I guessed he'd never been to Greenhill. He poured out glasses of bitter lemon for me and Julie and little cups of coffee for my parents. He invited us all to sit on the low canvas chairs with the bright woven cushions on them. He passed around a plate of small flat cookies dotted with nuts and raisins and another of crackers spread with runny cheese. This was dessert? "You would think that everyone would want to keep our building the way it is." Mr. Partridge grinned his quick grin that had nothing to do with anything funny.

"Was the building always so elegant?" Mom sat back and crossed her legs in her old, confident, Greenhill style. I could almost see the pool over her shoulder.

"Oh, no, my dears! I had to work like a

beaver to get that lobby in shape. Every time I changed the merest light bulb, somebody went bananas." He took a sip of coffee. "But we have problems in this building that are far more serious than light bulbs." He set down his cup. "Some of our tenants would like to turn the place into a slum."

"That's hard to believe," my father said.

"It may be hard to believe, but you must believe me. I really feel I should warn you about the Kendals. That girl of theirs is out of control. She's undisciplined and troublesome! Last year she actually invited people from the welfare hotel up to their place for dinner. Some crack-brained idea for a school report. Fortunately, my daughter, Kiki, told me about it, and I was able to alert the board of directors. Now it seems she's at it again. I've warned the parents, but I have a feeling they encourage her. She endangers us all. I will have to take some sort of action." He sighed. "This is *so-o-o* unpleasant."

"I can just imagine." My mother was frowning from the effort to imagine it.

"So watch your daughters!" Mr. Partridge

shook his finger at us in a joking way that I didn't think was a joke. "And I'll watch mine. The city is a hard place to raise them."

Fruitcake suddenly shrieked from the balcony and plopped down on the back of Mr. Partridge's chair.

"How marvelous!" my mother exclaimed. "A parrot!"

"Poor thing. He misses Kiki when she's not here."

Mr. Partridge stroked Fruitcake's neck. "I got these creatures to round out my jungle look when *Home Magazine* came here to photograph, and somehow they all stayed."

Dad glanced over his shoulder. "All?"

"There's a monkey and two parakeets and one cockatoo. Plus Fruitcake, of course. I must confess I've grown fond of the menagerie. I wanted to explore the jungle theme in color and design." He gestured grandly. "Lush greens and deep earth tones, subtle plays of leaf and fern, tree and sky. The animals have been an important ingredient. As *Home Magazine* described the style, it's safari mixed with urban elegance."

My parents admired the furniture and the plants and the rugs and pillows—and the coffee and crackers and cheese—as if we'd spent our lives in a cave on a mountaintop. Why were they so impressed? Didn't they remember where we had lived in Greenhill? When they were practically worn out from oohing and aahing, we went home.

The minute our door was closed my father said, "Alison, I want you to avoid K.J. Kendal."

"We don't need trouble in this building," Mom added. "The Kendals aren't our kind of people."

"What kind of people are they?"

"Oddballs," my father said.

I thought how I missed K.J. and how we had ideas in common. "Maybe I'm an oddball, too."

"*Avoid* her," Dad repeated.

"I know what!" Mom slid into her bright I'm-changing-the-subject tone of voice. "How about we do something together that's fun and exciting?" She looked around our foyer for an idea. "We don't live in a jungle like our neighbor, but we can visit one."

The next morning Mom, Julie, and I set off for the Bronx Zoo. The day was bright and cool. The city seemed flooded with sunlight. We took the crosstown bus and then an express bus right up to the gate. Once on the zoo grounds, if you were careful not to look up high enough to see the tops of apartment buildings over the trees, you could imagine you were in the wild. I had only been to the small zoo in Central Park, so I was surprised by the large fields with amazing birds strutting around in them. There was a twisting path that led to an area surrounded by a fence. This was like a park with animals.

Julie kept pointing excitedly. "What's that? What's that?"

Not far away there was a giraffe, looking nearly as tall as the distant buildings. He arched his neck to chew on a bunch of leaves. Near him, sitting perfectly still on a small brown hill, was a beautiful doglike cat with a graceful, long body covered with spots. He was staring at me. His eyes were gentle and shy.

"It's a cheetah." My mother read from a glass-encased sheet near the fence. "World's fastest sprinter. They inhabit the African plains. People in India trained them to hunt deer and hares. Pharaohs in ancient Egypt trained them to hunt wild game."

"He looks familiar," I said.

"Maybe he reminds you of that ginger cat we had, Molly. She was the same color," Mom said. "Cheetahs are illegal to keep as pets. You could only have seen him in a zoo or a book."

We moved on to see the baby elephant and the rhinoceros. Then Julie rode on the back of the camel. I felt a million miles away from K.J. and Rochelle and Jasper and Mr. Partridge—and from that jittery feeling of starting at a new school. But on the express bus going home we passed miles of empty broken-down buildings—boarded up, strewn with rubble—and I thought of the animals in the zoo and the people sleeping on Broadway and the cheetah I knew I had seen before. I remembered: it was the statue in Mr. Partridge's study.

When we got off the bus at our stop a woman came toward us. She couldn't seem to walk straight. Her eyes were filmy. "I need money," she said to Mom. "Got any change?"

My mother gripped both Julie and me by the wrists and kept walking. Julie began to suck her thumb. I tried Rochelle's tough expression. My mother glared at the sidewalk. "In case you're wondering," she said through her teeth, "I am not giving money to anybody who will go out and spend it on drugs."

"Someone should give her something for food, though," I said.

"Someone should, but not me and not a couple of eleven-year-old do-gooders."

"It was my can and I'm seven," Julie reminded her.

"OK, OK." Mom let go of us. I thought she wanted to put her hands over her ears. "We didn't have to see all this stuff in Greenhill."

"That didn't mean it wasn't there." I knew I sounded like K.J. Again.

"Look, Alison." Mom stopped walking. "I have enough on my mind. Do you think I enjoyed losing my job and watching Dad lose his job? Do you think I loved all those months till he could find another one? I know I told you moving into the city would be an adventure for our family, but that was baloney. It is a nightmare. I have been as brave as I know how to be. Don't push me, OK?" She chopped the air with her hand as if I actually were about to push her. I could see her nails hadn't been manicured. In Greenhill, she had had a standing appointment.

We crossed Broadway. On the island in the middle of the street was the bench with the sleeping man who had his feet sticking out of a paper carton. "This is the limit," my mother exploded. "Somebody ought to do something about this!"

At dinner, we told my father about the zoo.

"I'd take your uptown zoo over my downtown zoo in a minute," he tried to joke.

"There's a midtown zoo, too," Mom said glumly, "and we're living in it."

Dad looked down at his plate.

"It's not your fault." My mother put her hand on his arm. "We just have to get used to it." She shook her head as if she were disagreeing with what she'd just said. "People begging two to a block, some of them mentally ill, some of them addicts, some of them just down and out. Why should we get used to it?"

My father looked up. "We can't move again, Susan."

"I know," Mom said. "It's not as if there's anything we can do."

"It's hopeless."

"Impossible."

Gloom settled about us like a fog. The dining room felt cramped. The air seemed heavy. Our pretty Greenhill furniture sat around like guests at the wrong party.

After dinner Julie and I watched a show on TV, but she couldn't follow it and I didn't feel like explaining everything. I called Rosemary.

"Oh gosh, Alison, we're starting school before you know it. We'll have Mrs. Murray this year, and the play will be *Our Town*. I hope I get the part of Emily.

"If it were dance, it would be different. I'm nervous with a straight acting part. Tina wants to work on the sets. Jessie is trying to organize baby-sitting jobs. Of course, Lisa is thrilled that she has her horse."

"I remember—Twinkle."

"We guess we ought to vote for a new president of the A-Ones since . . ."

"Since I'm not there anymore." I finished her sentence.

"It's hard for you to keep coming to meetings," Rosemary said.

"And I have lots of things to do here."

"Oh, good." She sounded relieved.

When I hung up, I looked at the phone for a while. It was OK if they voted for a new president, even though the A-Ones were my idea. I *did* have lots of things to do. Like what? Like calling Jasper back again. I dialed the number.

"I've been looking for you," Jasper said. "I just missed you at the pool, and when I called, you never called me back."

"I called back yesterday. K.J. told me you were out."

"She's too proud to tell you how she wishes you'd be her friend again."

"Is that why you called? To tell me that?"

"I called to ask if we could go swimming together. I could meet you in the lobby. Next Monday. Around ten.

"Around ten," I repeated. "Sounds OK."

I hung up. Suddenly the apartment was full of sunlight. It seemed huge.

I went to our room. My side of the partition was like a warm little nest. The yellow-and-blue summer quilt on my bed showed up better than it had in Greenhill, where my room was so big. Even Julie's mess seemed cozy.

Later, my parents came in to say good night—first to me and then to Julie. I heard Julie's loud kiss.

"Good night, pumpkin," Dad said.

"If you lose your job again," Julie asked, "would we be homeless?"

My father laughed a big *ha-ha-ha*. "Oh, heavens no!"

"Why not?"

"We have loads of people who would help us out. Grandma and Grandpa and Aunt Helen and Uncle Robert and lots and lots more."

"Maybe tomorrow somebody will help all those people on the street."

"Maybe," Dad said. "Anything's possible."

In the morning my mother broke her last nail and clipped the others. "Manicured nails are a hobby I can't afford anymore," she decided. She filed them down. "Now all I've got to do is figure out how to pay the bills and do a load of wash and . . . Oh, Alison, could you take a box to the post office? Another jacket from L. L. Bean is not in my budget right now." She repacked the denim jacket she had sent away for and taped the box shut. "No more mail order. The returns run up an extra bill."

No more manicures. No more mail order. No more extra jackets.

I went out to the elevator with the box. No more tennis. No more country club. No more big house. No more A-Ones. I rang for the elevator and looked at myself in the hall mirror.

"No more no-mores," I told my reflection, and the words made me feel strange and free. It was as if I had taken off a tight old coat and could breathe deeply. It was time for something new to happen.

On the way to the post office I had an idea what the something new would be.

FIFTEEN

Next to the post office was the low red-brick building called the Uptown Interfaith Center, where K.J. had poured out glasses of juice. After I mailed off my mother's box I went up the stairs of the center. At the door a heavy man was asking each person what their business was.

"My friend told me this is a soup kitchen," I said. "I would like to help out."

"Here's a number to call." He wrote it

down on the back of a card. "They'll give you the information."

A man came up just behind me. "Can I get in?" he mumbled.

"You're too late, Charlie. You have to be here by ten-thirty if you want lunch."

"Could I get something?"

"Not today."

I took the number and ran all the way home.

"What's the matter with you, Alison?" My mother looked alarmed when I came in the door. "You're all red. Is the fever back?"

"I have to make a phone call." I dialed the number on the card. I spoke to a woman named Mrs. Dabney.

"You would have to be here by ten on a Tuesday or Thursday morning," she told me. "You won't be allowed in the dining room, but we could use your help in the kitchen, preparing sandwiches and setting up trays. You have to be accompanied by a parent or another adult if you're under eighteen."

When I hung up, my mother raised her eyebrows. "What was that all about?"

"A surprise," I said.

"Hmmm." She frowned. "I'm not very good at surprises."

I crossed my fingers and hoped she'd be good at this one.

The afternoon heat made it almost too hot to move. We turned on the air conditioner in my parents' room, and I started another book off the Ogilvey summer reading list. It was hard to concentrate. I had to read each sentence over a couple of times. All I could think about was my plan.

My mother said it was too hot to cook. She sent me down with Julie to pick up some salads from the deli.

"What would you like?" the deli man asked me when it was my turn.

"Something that will put my parents in the mood to say 'yes.' "

"Volunteer in a soup kitchen?" My father dropped his fork into the tri-colored pasta salad with pesto sauce and gaped at me.

My mother stopped chewing.

I thought, *Maybe I should have bought the*

potato salad and sliced steak. "Kids can't work in the dining room until we're eighteen," I said fast. "But we can help out in the kitchen making sandwiches and fixing trays."

"You?"

"And you, too, Mom. You would be the accompanying adult."

"You and me?" My mother stared at the table mat. "I don't believe this," she told it.

"And maybe K.J. and Rochelle," I said. "Rochelle's actually been there with her class. She told me about it."

"Rochelle Braden told you about it?" My father suddenly found his voice again. "Now I've heard everything."

"We could all go together." I laughed cheerily, like we were discussing a trip to the ice capades. "Day after tomorrow."

"What about Julie?" Julie asked.

"You could be the accompanying child," I told her.

My mother put her face in her hands.

"You told me I would find new friends and new clubs," I reminded her.

She turned to my father. "In Greenhill I

took them to swimming meets and sailing classes. Now I don't see why I shouldn't take them to the soup kitchen."

My father sighed, and then he actually smiled. "It's not Rolling Rock." He shook his head. "But maybe it's a club for where we are."

As soon as supper was over I called Rochelle. "My mother will take us to the Interfaith Center to volunteer. If you get your parents' permission, you can come, too, every Tuesday and Thursday."

"Sounds better than looking at old summer stuff on sale."

"We ought to get organized. My place tomorrow at eleven."

I called K.J. "Come to a meeting of my new club."

"I'm not interested in swimming and tennis. I hate clubs."

"This isn't swimming and tennis. It's a work-at-the-soup-kitchen and help-out-in-the-neighborhood club. Twice a week my mother will take us to the Interfaith Center so we can volunteer. We need other ideas for helping in this neighborhood. First meeting at my place, tomorrow at eleven."

"But I *hate* Rochelle."

"This is not a club for friendship. It is an organization for activists. Be here at eleven."

The next morning Julie decided we had to invite Kiki to our meeting. "She's across the hall for the whole week." Before I could stop her Julie was out the door ringing the Partridges' bell.

Kiki opened the door in her nightgown. She didn't say a word until Julie was finished describing what we wanted to do, then she frowned. "I'll have to check with Mrs. Marshall."

We followed her into the living room, where Mrs. Marshall was watching television. "The Interfaith Center soup kitchen? Good heavens, what an idea!" Mrs. Marshall snapped. "Mr. Partridge wouldn't even let Kiki go with her class last year. He would never consent to her being in that place."

"My mother will take us," I said.

"I don't care if Queen Elizabeth takes you.

It's out of the question. I won't allow it. Mr. Partridge won't allow it. Kiki is too young to see such things."

Kiki looked at the floor.

"She sees them on the street every day."

"We shield her from that sort of scene. That's my job." Mrs. Marshall got up and led us to the door.

Kiki still stared at the floor, but her neck was bright red. "I want to go, Mrs. Marshall," she called out in her flat voice.

"Oh, no you don't, dear. Believe me. Your father will say no." Mrs. Marshall opened the door to let us out. After she closed it, we heard the double lock click shut.

"I'm glad I don't have a nanny," Julie said.

When we got home I prepared for my meeting. I put four pencils and four pieces of notepaper around the dinette table. I was nervous about what Rochelle would say when she saw how we lived in half the space of her apartment. I wondered if K.J. would show up.

Rochelle rang our bell at 11:00 sharp. "I like your place," she told my mother right away. "It's so cozy."

"You should have seen our house in Greenhill," Mom sighed. "We could fit this whole apartment in our old living room."

"Let's start the meeting," I interrupted, before bragging mode could set in.

We sat around the dinette table, and I started the meeting. "Work in the soup kitchen is just one project. We should have other plans for the year."

"How about signing up volunteers at school?" Rochelle said. "We could post a list on the bulletin board. People could help collect cans of food and clothing for the center."

"How much money?" Julie held her can over her head.

Rochelle began to get excited. "There's a program. It's called Common Cents. You collect pennies door-to-door, like a penny harvest." She grinned at me. "Only we'd better get permission from our co-op board first."

"We got lots of money in my can last time." Julie opened her can and looked into it. "We bought food with the money. I'm really hungry."

"There's tri-colored pasta salad with pesto

sauce," I said. "Nobody ate it last night. If we don't finish it, we'll have it again tonight."

I began to put out the food. Julie took hold of my arm. "Is it our fabulous new life yet?" she whispered.

"Yes," I whispered back. "Absolutely."

After lunch we went up to Rochelle's to watch an old movie on the VCR in Mrs. Braden's air-conditioned den. It was Judy Garland and Mickey Rooney in black and white. The story was about a bunch of kids who try to put on a show. Even though the plot seemed corny and old-fashioned, the movie reminded me of our new club: it was about taking an idea and trying to make something real happen.

By the time the movie was over so was the afternoon. Julie and I took the stairs home. On the eighth-floor landing, we heard Kiki's voice coming from her apartment. I couldn't make out the words, but it sounded as if she was part talking and part crying.

"Let's see what's wrong." Julie rushed to the door.

"It's private." I pulled her back.

In the kitchen my mother was telling my father how she had called the center. "I told them to put us down for Tuesday and Thursday until school starts," Mom said.

"What about after school starts?" my father asked me.

"We have a list of other ideas we're working on," I told him. "Rochelle came up with some good ones."

"The Braden girl?" My father shook his head unbelievingly. I knew he was going to say, "Now I've heard everything." "Now I've heard everything," he said.

Our doorbell rang three sharp rings, one after the other, as if someone very angry was jabbing at it.

"What's this?" My mother looked alarmed.

We all trooped after her to find out.

I had a feeling we hadn't heard everything.

Sixteen

Mr. Partridge stood under the hall chandelier between our apartment and his. Kiki leaned on her door frame, just behind him. She wasn't wearing any shoes, and her eyes were pink rimmed, like a rabbit's.

"Sorry to bother you." Mr. Partridge flashed his white grin. "I've come to ask a little favor, Mrs. Fox. Would it be too much to request that you and your children *not* include Kiki in your plans."

"The girls thought she might want to join

us," Mom said. "I apologize for not asking you first."

"Exactly." He nodded. "Mrs. Marshall tells me the invitation caused Kiki quite an upset."

"I don't want Mrs. Marshall anymore," Kiki interrupted. "I'm too old for a nanny."

"Mrs. Marshall is an old friend," Mr. Partridge told Kiki over his shoulder.

"I have new friends," Kiki said.

Mr. Partridge shook his head and smiled sadly at my father. "See what I mean?"

"But wouldn't it be pleasant if the girls could be friendly?" My mother was in her Greenhill-charming mode.

"Not if some of them are given the freedom to break rules and make trouble."

"I don't break rules and make trouble, do I?" Julie pulled on my father's wrist.

"No." He patted Julie's head.

"No, no, no, no," Kiki repeated.

"Hush," Mr. Partridge told her.

"You hush!" Kiki burst out. We watched her take two long steps backward into the duplex and open the door to her father's

study. "You're the one who breaks the rules!" she cried. "King Tut's a rule-breaker."

A beautiful doglike cat strode through the door and sat down in the middle of the rug.

"He's in the dollhouse," Julie gasped.

"He's in the zoo, too," I said.

"He's an illegal endangered cheetah," my mother said. "What's he doing here?"

SEVENTEEN

Mr. Partridge took hold of the cheetah's gold collar. His fluorescent teeth flashed at me. Even though his face was red and miserable, he was trying to smile. "A friend thought he would be a nice addition to my jungle look."

"You object to my daughters raising money for poor people while you keep a cheetah in your apartment?" Dad said unbelievingly.

"King Tut has been happy here." Mr.

Partridge's voice was pleading. "He's tame. He's very fond of me."

"He's got to go," my father said. "I'm calling the ASPCA."

"Cheetahs are as shy and proud as they are beautiful." Mr. Partridge's voice was low and sad. "King Tut is no longer young. I could donate him to the children's zoo, perhaps." He shook his head and tried to smile again but couldn't. "The fact is, I'm very attached to him, and he is attached to me. Cheetahs don't form friendships easily. And when they do, they are unable to share their loyalty with ease." His eyes settled on King Tut. The cheetah gazed back at Mr. Partridge as if he were listening.

"There was one who turned against her young when she became upset by the crowds at the zoo," Mr. Partridge continued. "King Tut, he trusts me. He rests his head on my knee. He even sits on my lap! I hope wherever it is he must go, I am allowed to see him." He took a deep breath and turned to face Julie and me. "I didn't mean to come down hard on you girls. It wasn't my intention to make your lives difficult. Is there anything I can do to reverse the damage?"

"Could our friends see the cheetah?" I asked.

He threw up his arms as if he were surrendering a battle. "Why not? Call in the troops."

I ran back into our apartment and dialed the Kendals. "I have something to tell you, K.J." I said.

"I know, you've got a club."

"Mr. Partridge has a cheetah."

"A what?"

"Cheetahs are illegal. He'll have to get rid of it, but he's so mortified he's been caught, he says you can see it."

"I'm busy right now."

I called Rochelle.

"A cheetah?" She hollered the news to her parents. "We'll be right there."

Out on the landing, King Tut sat still as a statue, gazing with golden brown eyes at his keeper.

"I do so wish they'd change the laws," Mr. Partridge said. "Cheetahs may take a long time to befriend, but they are worth it."

Rochelle came out of the elevator with her parents just behind her. Just behind them was Jasper Kendal.

"I had to see this," Jasper explained, smiling at me.

"Awesome," Rochelle whispered.

I wondered if she was a mind reader until I realized she was describing King Tut, not Jasper.

"What a fabulous look," Mrs. Braden gushed over the cheetah. She turned to my parents. "I had a client who kept miniature pigs and another who had wild cats. Pigs, wild cats, cheetahs—what next?"

"Foxes?" My father put out his hand. "How do you do."

"Would anybody care for a glass of something cool?" My mother swung into her hostess mode. "I've got terrific lemonade."

I stopped her before she ran back to the kitchen. "This is Jasper Kendal."

"Jasper Kendal." Mom greeted him with a big smile. "I see."

"The lemonade's on the top shelf," she said. "How many glasses do we need, Jasper?"

"Ten," he counted. "And a large pet bowl."

At the top of the service stairs I saw something move.

"Don't look now," Jasper whispered. "There's your friend K.J."

"I won't look. She'd run away if I did."

He followed me into the kitchen.

"She's just impossible," Jasper said.

I took the pitcher of lemonade out of the refrigerator.

"No, she's not impossible. She just takes a long time to befriend," I said. "Like the cheetah."

I poured lemonade into glasses and handed them to Jasper, who put them on a tray. A couple of things occurred to me. For one, Jasper wasn't an Impossible any more. For another, life in New York was *really* looking up.

"What are you grinning about?" Jasper asked.

"You know that point in a swim meet when you can tell you aren't going to lose and you may even do better than your own best?"

"Yes." Jasper nodded. "It's when anything seems possible."

"That's what I'm grinning about." I took two glasses off the tray and handed one to him. "So here's to it," I said.

"Here's to what?" Jasper asked.

"Possibilities," I said.